The Void

By Kyle Berkley

Published By:
Bold Print Publishing

Bold Print Publishing • info@KyleSBerkley.com

Ordering Information:
Quantity sales. Special discounts are available on quantity purchases by corporations, associations, and others. For details, contact the publisher at the address above.

Orders by U.S. trade bookstores and wholesalers.
Please contact info@KyleSBerkley.com

Book Cover Artwork by: K&T Graphic Designs
Edited by: Karen Rodgers

ISBN: 979-8-9877806-0-2
Copyright © 2023 Kyle S. Berkley
All rights reserved

Dedication

This book is dedicated to my father, Samuel Berkley, my uncle Elisha Garland, my cousin Kenneth Bowman, and my best friend Chris Burton. This book is also dedicated to the life and memories of Antonio Washington, aka Tony Bones, and so many other brothers and sisters we have lost over the years.

Acknowledgments

Before I start, I would like to state this Acknowledgments section will be a lot shorter than the one that appears in *The Wake*. Not because nothing has changed, but because there were a lot of names.

I first want to give all thanks and praise to my creator. Without Him, all the great things I have accomplished would not have happened. A kid from West Port, Baltimore City that has published books, and graduated college with a Ph.D.! WOW! I have to give thanks to my loving and supportive wife, my three beautiful daughters, Savannah, Sage, and Shiloh. I wish I could put hearts by all of their names. They're my whole world. I also have to thank my parents for all they have poured into me to become the man I am today.

My sisters Kyrissa, Kim, Toi, and Brenda. My brothers Lamont, Andre, Anthony, Angelo, Charles, John Mark, and Reggie. I would like to give special thanks to my family and friends that have helped me throughout my life. I'm trying to keep this short without saying too many names because I don't want to forget anybody.

I genuinely love you all. I can't move past this section without giving thanks to the lawyers that gave me so much input into certain chapters of this story and the next (yes, the follow-up to this story, *The Legacy* will be out shortly). I also want to thank Cheryl Barton along with each and every person that purchased *The Wake*. It meant so much to have my book supported and promoted the way it was and to arrive at this place.

Table of Contents

Prelude

Previously in *The Wake*, Titan Industries, led by siblings Chandler and Chanel Titan along with the wealthy married couple Erica and Sedrick Little, began revitalizing the West Baltimore City Community, Ridgely Square. In the course of re-imagining Ridgely Square, many residents faced displacement, and the majority of the current residents learned they would not be able to afford to live in the new and improved Ridgely Square.

Pastor Donald Avery and Florence Simms, long-time Ridgely Square community leaders, fought against the proposed gentrification that the community faced from Titan Industries, along with terminal health challenges. Pastor Avery searched for a person who could lead his financially struggling New Hope Greater Love Church along with Ridgely Square before succumbing to his illness.

Tina Simms is the granddaughter of Florence Simms, and her father, Larry Simms, was a Baltimore City school teacher that was murdered during a robbery while leaving his job. Tina's mother, Gina Simms, was estranged from Larry and Tina due to her substance abuse. Tina would soon move in with Florence Simms's daughter, Linda, and son-in-law Daryl "Cube" Gibbons. Tina would also begin a relationship with her classmate, a high school football star, named Tyrone Clinton. While living with her aunt and uncle, Tina was sexually assaulted by her uncle Daryl and she would later take her own life.

Tyrone Clinton grew up in a single-parent household with his mother, Sasha Greene. Like Tina Simms, Tyrone was a senior and a standout football player, scouted by several colleges. Tyrone was suspended from school athletics due to a decline in his grades. He made a deal with his football coach, Edward Carter, who also worked as a Baltimore City police officer, that he would improve his grades. As part of the agreement, Edward said if Tyrone made the honor roll, he would let Tyrone drive his car to the prom with Tina Simms. While leaving the library one day, a young man, who was involved in one of the local gangs and ran a betting racket, forced Tyrone Clinton to rob a pizza carryout. During the course of the robbery, Tyrone was shot and killed by Officers Lake and Moreland. The two officers never faced punishment for the shooting, even after video evidence showed that Tyrone Clinton gave himself up during the course of the arrest.

Following the death of Tyrone Clinton, several groups in the community began to protest and riot. This led the Baltimore City Police Commissioner, Alex Tillman, to defend his officers' actions, along with being questioned about his policing practices by community leader Minister Hakeem Andrews. While speaking with fellow officer Stone about proposing to his girlfriend, Officer Edward Carter and Officer Stone witnessed a young man by the name of Kennard Lyles-Bey spray painting a wall. Upon his approach, Kennard attempted to show Edward Carter, who he recognized as a football coach, the final report card of his deceased friend Tyrone Clinton. Reacting quickly and in fear of Kennard reaching into his pocket, Officer Stone shot Kennard. At the hospital, Edward Carter attempted to see Kennard and his family to apologize, but he was ordered by Commissioner Tillman to return home. Before Edward Carter could leave, a group of men shot at Edward Carter and Commissioner Alex Tillman. The police

Commissioner returned fire, killing the two men, but Edward Carter also died during the exchange.

Silk Diamond was a former radio personality, born Simon Little, to her parents, Erica and Sedrick Little. At an early age, Silk witnessed her sister die during a hit-and-run. After years of battling with her sexuality, she moved out of her parents' home and pursued a career in entertainment. Her career in entertainment was cut short after sleeping with the husband of the owner of the radio station and she was terminated from the radio station. Silk subsequently faced difficulty locating employment as a transwoman. She became homeless and began sex work for income before befriending a longtime sex worker, Gina Simms. One night Silk was meeting with a regular customer, Daryl Gibbons, who was angry that he contracted HIV from Silk in a previous session. That night Daryl killed Silk in retaliation. Silk's parents had a closed funeral for her under her born name, Simon Little. That became a major point of contention when Gina Simms saw the name posted in the funeral home when she was paying her final respects to her own daughter, Tina.

Tiffany Simms, a beautiful 5 foot 6 inch African American woman at 33 years old was the oldest granddaughter to Florence Simms, who had a lengthy battle with Alzheimer's disease. Tiffany lived with her five children, Desha, Darrin, RJ, Trinity, and Kenya and her boyfriend Keyon. Tiffany and Keyon went through a bad breakup when Keyon gave up his search for employment and began staying home smoking marijuana all day. After getting put out of their apartment, Keyon began working as a custodian for Pastor Avery's New Hope Greater Love Church and even stayed in a room in the church for a period of time. During that time Tiffany learned that Titan had purchased the apartment building she and Sasha

Greene lived in, which would soon be demolished and displace them. One day while visiting her grandmother, Florence Simms, in the hospital Tiffany learned that Kenya and Keyon were involved in a hit-and-run that would soon take their lives. Following the death of Florence Simms, Tiffany learned that she was willed the family home. She would soon learn what voids were left behind by the people Ridgely Square lost in 2016.

Chapter 1

On a beautiful spring afternoon in the Ridgley Square community of Baltimore City, Maryland, several people are gathered in the Allen Bradley Funeral Home. The people gathered are seated in a circle discussing their grief over the loss of their loved ones. The Ridgely Square community has faced a spike in murders over the last four months, following the deaths of two African American teenagers at the hands of the Baltimore City police. The first, Tyrone Clinton was shot and killed during a botched robbery, and the second was Kennard Lyles-Bey, who was accidentally shot by a Baltimore City police officer and died several days later in the hospital. I take a deep breath to slow the rapid beating of my heart. I can feel my hands shaking, they won't stop moving because I know it's time to share with the group. Something I have avoided for weeks, speaking to others about my grief and my life.

"You can speak whenever you're ready," Ms. Toya says with a warm look. She is a medium-built African American woman in her early 50s. She grew up in the Ridgley Square community. My grandmother, Florence Simms, used to babysit her. Allen Bradley decided it was best for her to run the grief counseling groups here at the funeral home because of her background in counseling. I tried to run one group and nearly had a nervous breakdown. I think they call it countertransference when the counselor is in some way emotionally affected by the person they are counseling.

"Hi everyone, my name is Tiffany. My daughter Kenya died in a car accident back in December. There's a lot about the accident I'm still not sure about. I remember it like it was yesterday. It kind of haunts me. I was with my cousin Tina in the hospital with my grandmother when I got the call from the emergency room that Kenya was downstairs. I still remember the tubes and the staff and everything. I have dreams about her every night. I also have dreams about my cousin Tina, who took her own life around the same time. I'm trying to move forward and be normal, but it's hard. Why am I here and they're not? I'm trying to figure it out. I have four other kids: my 11-year-old twins Desha and Darrin, my 9-year-old daughter Trinity and my 8-year-old son RJ."

I stop talking for a second, I look at some of the faces in the group and realize I don't know these people. I see them every week, but I don't know them. I hear their stories, but I don't know them. Are they judging me for being a bad mother? Do they think I'm fat? Do they think I'm ugly? Do they think I'm a hoe for having so many children and never being married? Should I keep talking? It is killing me to keep these feelings within. I should continue, but I can feel my heart beating harder and harder. I can feel the breath leaving out of me before I can exhale. What is wrong with me? Why am I scared of these strangers? I ignore the rest of my mental ramblings and take a deep breath. I picture my daughter Kenya and push past the grief.

"I had to bury my daughter." I just blurt that out. No real thought behind it, I just tell everyone that. "Kenya… I had to bury her. It was hard to do. I used the money from my student refund and some money that was donated and buried her. It was the hardest thing I ever had to do. I had no support, my grandmother died around the same time, she was in the viewing room up the hall. My cousin Tina, who took her own life, was in this viewing room and Kenya's father was also dead. He died in a car accident with Kenya. The detectives told me it was a hit-and-run, but for all I know, they could have been the ones that caused the hit-and-run. They get away with so much around here, and we just suffer. My daughter didn't deserve to die. I'm fearful that any of my other kids could be next. Nobody helps me with them, I don't want or need the help, but Keyon, Kenya's father was a man that provided for his child. I was so proud of the man he was becoming, then *boom*. My life changed, my baby girl was taken from me, and it wasn't his fault."

Was it my fault for breaking up with him when he didn't have a job? Was it my fault for putting him out of the house when I caught him with weed, and he didn't purchase milk and groceries? Was it my fault for calling the police on him when he was fighting my new boyfriend? What was his name? Oh yeah, Tony. He was so annoying, and he had the worst smelling feet.

"I have had difficulty focusing, like in school. I changed my major from nursing to social work. Not sure why, but I feel like it's something I'm interested in. Helping people that need help. I'm working at Ridgely Square Hospital. I'm trying to provide for the kids. It's easier not having to pay rent, thank God my grandmother left us the house. I feel like I'm rambling, I apologize. It's been like this for a while with me. My mind won't shut off. I forget to eat most days, and I can't sleep. I'm sorry y'all I've said too much."

Ms. Toya glances at me with a sympathetic smile as other members in the group tear up. "It's ok, we've been there before," one of the other women in the group says as Ms. Toya starts talking. I notice my aunt Gina changing her posture in her chair and is anxious to speak. Though I will never tell her, she is a beautiful dark-skinned woman. She even has a nice wig on today. She has been in recovery for her drug addiction for several months. We are not on the best of terms, but she has been trying to connect with me since the death of her daughter Tina back in December.

"Hi everyone, my name is Gina. My beautiful and super intelligent niece Tiffany shared that my daughter Tina took her life back in December. Something I've been coming to grips with is how I failed her and my family with the choices I've made in life. My husband was killed last year during a robbery at his job. I wasn't there for the funeral, the planning, or in his life prior to. Why? Because I was out getting high and sex working. My mother-in-law Florence helped raise my daughter, along with Tiffany. Looking back on everything now, it's embarrassing. You can't get that time back. You can't get those lives back.

"There's a lot of memories that Tiffany has with my daughter, with my husband and with my niece, Kenya, I never got to experience. Because of my choices. I missed my daughter going to middle school, high school, talking to boys, going to prom, and making great grades. I messed up. I could have gone to treatment at any time. But I wanted to have fun and be free. Free from responsibilities. I felt like I was tied down to vows, and parenthood. The lightbulb went off when I met a young transwoman that was out sex working and homeless. This girl had issues with her parents and life dealt her an unfair hand. Then I thought about my little girl, and before I could do anything, she took her life. I can't help but think I was the reason she did it."

Aunt Gina begins to cry as two of the members of the group embrace her. I swear she's good. She can get a rise out of anybody. Should I buy into this crap? I guess she has been there for me more than my own mother. Gina would win the Nobel Peace Prize in comparison to my parents. My mother was an enabler, and my father was a molester. He raped me and he raped Tina. I know that's the reason why Tina killed herself. I wonder how well Aunt Gina has been able to process that? How do sex workers process rape and sexual assault? Is it the same as a person like me, or is the processing barrier different? I ask because well… their livelihood is sex. Here I go drifting off into a random ponder while this group goes on. I wonder how much time is left; never mind, I see the group is over.

"Hey Tiffany," Gina says, coming in my direction. She never stops trying to bond with me. "Do you mind if I walk home with you?"

"You're going to do it anyway," I bark. "Why do you always do that? You act like we're friends or something."

"We are family, remember? I am your aunt. But I apologize. I really am trying to build a relationship with you. You're all I have left."

"Fine," I respond, knowing that she's being genuine. "How are you settling in at home?"

As we walk out of the funeral home and onto the bright sunny streets of Baltimore City, we are greeted with the smell of cigarette smoke and car exhaust fumes. My house is about two blocks up the road. Gina recently moved back into the house that she and her deceased husband Larry, used to own. My mother illegally sold the house to a company called Titan Industries to pay my grandmother's hospital bills. Gina threatened to take Titan to court over the sale, and they awarded her back the home along with a nice chunk of cash to keep quiet.

"It's ok, lonely but ok," Gina answers, looking at her cell phone.

"How are you doing with the groups and everything? I know you have been talking about your past a lot in the documentary you're recording." My aunt Gina was a major reason why the community reconstruction project stopped. Right place, right time. A big news story broke, and she was able to seize the moment with the state's attorney turned news analyst, Anna Cartwright. Anna recently started recording my aunt for an upcoming documentary on substance abuse and sex work in Baltimore City. Though I will never admit it, I'm scared that all the pressure of success could lead to her relapsing. Think about it, house, financial settlement and getting money from a documentary. Too much of a good thing has to turn bad at some point, right? Maybe I'm just being negative.

"I'm ok, Tiffany, trust me. If I couldn't handle this, I would stop, but is she ok?" Gina asks, pointing at Sasha drinking on the top stone step leading to my front door. Sasha used to live in the apartment building I lived in until Titan Industries purchased the complex and displaced us. When my grandmother gifted me her house, I offered Sasha a place to stay for a short period of time. The least I could do after her son, Tyrone Clinton, was shot and killed by a police officer. The boy was caught robbing a carryout, he gave himself up and still was killed. She has been handling his death horribly.

"Sasha. Sasha! What the hell, Sasha," I yell at her while she drinks a 22-ounce bottle of Bud Ice. Three other empty bottles, along with two miniature bottles of tequila lay next to her on the step. The police could have easily locked her up for drinking outside. Aside from that, my kids could have seen her like this. "Is this why you didn't go to work last night?"

"What," Sasha answers back in her loud raspy voice. She reeks of cigarette smoke and alcohol. "I ain't hurt nobody or bother nobody. Where have you been?"

"We were at the grief group, where you should have been," I respond. I fear the alcohol smell could cause Gina to relapse.

As Sasha falls over on her right side, Gina and I run to help her up and carry her inside the house. "You got to cut back on this drinking, girl," Gina says to an inebriated Sasha, concern lining her face.

I tell my aunt Gina, "Shut up, you just got clean last week. Nobody needs your sermons."

"Oh, and you're better? Where are your kids, Tiffany? When was the last time you helped them with their homework?" Sasha mumbles as we help her to the brown recliner in the living room.

"Where *are* my kids?" I ask, concerned that Sasha did something neglectful to my children.

"Hakeem has them at the community center," Sasha says in a faint tone before nodding off to sleep. My boyfriend Hakeem has been super helpful with the kids in recent weeks. "You need to meet with the school counselor, Desha and RJ must have done something. They both have letters from the counselor." Sasha smirked after delivering her proof of my neglect.

Great, this counselor has been sending letters home for the kids for the last couple of weeks. Today just couldn't get any worse. Sasha is pissy drunk on my grandmother's recliner and Gina is in my grandmother's house. My grandmother did not want Gina to set foot in this house again, especially after she stole items back when I was younger. My grandmother never got over Gina leaving my uncle Larry to be a prostitute and do drugs. I guess I'll add allowing Gina to enter my grandmother's home, against her dying wishes, to the list of things I got wrong in life.

Chapter 2

I left Gina with Sasha at the house and went to get the kids from the community center, located a block up the street from the house. Of course, there's a lot of gang activity around here, and I can't walk 5 steps without somebody's son trying to talk to me and then calling me out my name for not wanting to give him my number. I'm really surprised that isn't a murderable offense, the way they are killing everybody in this community. Walking through the community center I see the basketball court and the classrooms. One classroom has my children watching videos on the computer, another has the brown-skinned, slim built Hakeem Andrews talking to a group of eight adults.

"Burnout is the thing we should all attempt to avoid," he says with his seductive baritone voice. He always speaks in a calm tone, even when he is mad. He has great control of his emotions. I guess that comes with years of advocating for rights and fighting inequality in Baltimore City. He is the founder and CEO of the advocacy group, Justice for All.

"Last year the city of Baltimore had a total of 318 murders. So far this year, we have had 124 murders in the city. Forty-one of the murder victims were from the Ridgley Square community. How does that affect you all? You go to work and deal with the stress and challenges from your jobs, then you come back to this community.

How do you process the murders?" Hakeem asks, looking across the room.

"I don't really think about it," a light-brown-skinned woman answers, looking at Hakeem. She appears to be in her mid-twenties. She has several colorful tattoos on her arms and on her neck. "I have lived here my whole life. Things have gotten worse over the last year, but what can you do?"

"So it sounds like you have normalized the murders and accepted the circumstances," Hakeem responds to the young woman.

"I mean what can we do? The police are just as bad as the gangs around here. Nothing is going to change. The politicians haven't done a thing to improve this neighborhood. We have more vacant houses now than we did last year this time. They want me to be happy about $15 an hour at my job, but I barely get decent hours, and I have to pay for transportation to get there and back. Food is high, both my sons have asthma, and I can barely afford their medication. It is what it is. I can't be concerned with the murders when life is killing me."

"So what do you do to keep yourself from being concerned with the murders?" Hakeem asks. The woman looks annoyed.

"I raise my sons, I try not to get shot, and I work," she responds with a curt tone.

"How do you relax, after managing to work, balance transportation, food, and medication costs? How do you relax?" Hakeem questions.

"I don't. It's my normal. I don't have the money to do anything. I want to go to the gym they have around the corner, but who can afford a new bill? I want to take the boys to a theme park, but who can afford that? The boys want to play sports, but the equipment costs money, along with the league fees. I work, come home, and parent. I would love to go to a bar or go to a club, but I don't have that type of freedom."

I get her perspective, I was literally in the same boat. When Kenya's father went through his stint of unemployment, I had to work twice as hard to cover for him and the five kids. I can feel her pain. Some people just don't get the luxury of self-care. Not when kids and rent come first. I wonder how much sleep she gets a night.

"I would encourage you all to watch a show, eat some ice cream, take a nap, or read a book. Do something for yourself this week, and let's talk about it during the next meeting. Have a good one, ladies," Hakeem says with a warm smile on his face as the participants walk out of the room. "Well that went worse than expected," Hakeem says jokingly as he turns towards me.

"All things considered, I think that went better than my experiment at being a grief counselor," I answer. "I still can't believe I had a breakdown and started crying while conducting the group. I would have made a horrible counselor."

"It's trauma," Hakeem blurts out. "She's numb because of compound trauma. Think about the constant murders, challenges with employment, and the cost of living. It's all traumatic. People are trying to cope, and I'm doing all I can to help, but I don't feel like I'm really making a difference."

"Maybe the difference you're trying to make is bigger than you," I answer, but Hakeem shakes his head in denial. "You can't stop the murder rate, improve the cost of living and provide insight for relaxing from life stressors. I could have easily been her. I might still be, now that I think about it."

As Hakeem opens his mouth to respond, a tall, very well built bearded man walks into the room wearing a blue suit with an unbuttoned shirt. It's Allen, the owner of the Allen Bradley Funeral Home. He and Hakeem have been working together for several months trying to improve the community. "Sorry to interrupt," Allen says in a soft tone, but his voice still booms and echoes in the room. "Have you heard that Ridgely Square Elementary School is closing at the end of the school year?"

"Yeah, the city council voted to defund the school, not sure if it's Titan Industries still trying to complete the community project or not," Hakeem answers. I should probably get the kids and head home; I do not need to think about this right now.

"It's a bidding war between Titan Industries and West Baltimore Hospital," Allen responds showing Hakeem a flyer. "They are now offering homeowners money for their homes."

"I swear we just went through this last year with Titan," I say, interrupting. Just last year Titan Industries attempted to purchase all of the homes in Ridgely Square with the goal of opening a planned community. They purchased the apartment complex I lived in and made everybody move out.

"Have you spoken to your brother Jamar about addressing this?" Allen asks. Hakeem and his brother aren't close. Hakeem and Jamar often bump heads on politics and religion. If Hakeem could have his way, he would avoid talking to Jamar altogether. As Hakeem shakes his head from left to right, Allen responds, "We need every resource possible. I need you to talk to Jamar."

Chapter 3

After dropping off the children at home, Hakeem and I walk inside a building that used to be a warehouse years ago that is currently being used as a community resource center. We are soon met by a man that looks almost identical to Hakeem, aside from having a scar along his right cheek that starts right below his eye. The man is very imposing and in very good shape. He is Hakeem's brother Jamar.

"Good afternoon, my sister," Jamar greets me. He is very polite and has always prided himself on treating women with honor. "Long time no hear from, Hakeem. What brings you in here today? Are you about to tell me that the police shot and killed another one of my youth?"

A lot of the newly harbored anger Jamar has towards Hakeem is related to the murder of Kennard Lyles-Bey, who was one of the youths that were in Jamar's boxing and mentorship classes at the community center.

"No, I would like to talk to you about helping with improving the community," Hakeem answers, making little eye contact with his brother. This is really awkward.

Hakeem continues to talk as Jamar relaxes his stance. "Titan is building in our community, Ridgley Square Hospital is losing funding and West Baltimore Hospital is attempting to purchase everything that Titan hasn't purchased. On top of that, several hospitals are doing all kinds of paid experimental medical research in our community, and our people are falling for it. Last year the West Baltimore Hospital did a test with an opioid that would reduce new onset substance abuse, post the completion of pain management. That drug led to more people seeking drugs in Ridgely Square. The increase in people seeking drugs in Ridgely Square led to the gangs getting out of control."

Jamar interrupts Hakeem with a sarcastic look. "The gangs! You want to talk about the gangs here? What about the police? I told you three years ago when you were getting traction with Justice for All, we should start our own police department and take control of our community. You were scared. You thought it excluded the city. Where did that get you? You want to talk about the gangs? If the police that are killing our youth did their jobs, they would arrest how many kids? How many of the kids I work with here would have a second chance at life without being labeled a felon, or go through the court system? I wanted you to help me with establishing our own police department because we could save our people. We could reduce crime because we know the problems that we face. Laws in this city don't fix systemic problems, they just add wrinkles to the ongoing flow of oppression."

"What is your plan, Jamar," Hakeem asks, clearly agitated with his brother.

"We purchase every home in the community that we can, we patrol with our own people, we give skills to every able-bodied citizen in Ridgely Square. We can provide affordable housing to those with low income. We can give housing to the homeless and people returning home from war and prison. We can get rid of anyone that is not like us or a part of the place we create," Jamar answers in a very frank tone. Jamar then invites us into a room and sits down, we follow suit.

"So you want to exclude people of different races?" I ask, feeling uncomfortable with Jamar's last statement.

"Yes, you have to get rid of the impurities. Who killed Tyrone Clinton, who killed Kennard Lyles-Bey? Police. What system do the police serve? They serve the system set in place that had us enslaved for 400 years. They serve the system that deconstructed the black family using public assistance programs. They serve the system that decides for us what is right and what is wrong. If I start a company without a business license, I have to pay the government for my creation. The police enforce that. If a sister at my mosque is assaulted by her husband on a nightly basis and the sister defends herself, it is the police's job to sort and charge based on their assessment. How many times have you seen the woman, who was the victim, get charged for defending herself? If we have our own police department, problems like that would not leave this community. We would handle it. How many murders go unsolved, Hakeem? If we were the eyes and ears, we would know and we would solve. We could stop the murders. We could reduce gang activity because we would know what led these young people to join the gangs to start with. The police react, we can prevent. Do you understand what I'm saying?"

"I think I do," Hakeem responds.

"When the police come to evict someone from their house or apartment for not paying rent, our police could make sure things don't get that far. You have a food pantry, right? How many of the people do you serve come every week? What skills do you mandate your recipients acquire to make sure they don't come back? You give them a meal, they will come back to eat again. If you show them how to obtain food and prepare the meal, they can do better for themselves. This is what I teach, and this is why my work here has been successful. If you need my help, what is the future you want to build for our people? I want our people to own every carryout in Ridgely Square and to only purchase from our people. I don't give a damn about anyone else," Jamar says, leaning forward. The way he pronounces his words is alluring.

"I think we can meet in the middle of this, Jamar," Hakeem responds nervously.

"There is no middle ground, my brother. You can't hold on to religious convictions, political party lines, or old systems that have never benefited us. It is time now to act. There is a group of police called NAFA, the Narcotics and Firearms Task Force that has been running Ridgley Square like the wild west for the last few months. We can blame the deaths on the gangs, but if you look at what NAFA has been doing, you'll see they have been pulling the strings," Jamar says, looking at me with sincerity in his eyes. "People here are barely surviving. We have to do better than survive. We have to thrive. Martin Luther King Jr begged, Jesse Jackson begged, Al Sharpton begged, I see you and your organization mean well, but you're begging. We have to take charge, seize what we want and thrive. The only way we can live in the Promised Land is to remove the natives that are currently living there."

Chapter 4

My aunt Gina, has been recording for a documentary on the Nubian Radio and Television Broadcasting Network for a couple of weeks, and for reasons I can't understand, she wants me to attend the filming sessions. Nubian started out as a radio broadcasting company, founded by the great Ms. Clair Hall and recently turned into an online streaming service for television content, with live news, television shows, podcasts, and movies. Aunt Gina's documentary has become a highly rated show among all streaming services and network television. Anna Cartwright, a former district attorney from Tennessee has been conducting the interviews with my aunt from the start. Two opportunists with a common goal, what could go wrong?

The recording studio is huge, with the shiniest wooden floors I have ever seen in my life. There are cameras and soundboards throughout the room, along with screens, monitors and set pieces. Gina is sitting on a set with Anna that has beautiful flowers and comfortable looking white chairs to provide a relaxed environment for guests. There is a beautiful table set between the two chairs, one seating Gina and the other seating Anna. Anna has blonde hair, blue eyes and dresses like a television evangelist from the 1980s. Gina is dressed in jeans and a button-up shirt, with the same wig on from earlier today. She's really beautiful.

"Gina, let's bring some of our listeners up to speed. If you don't mind, please tell us about your past," Anna asks with her southern drawl.

"Well, I was an active crack cocaine and heroin user for decades. I went from having a future in journalism to being a sex worker. I destroyed relationships with family, friends, and colleagues," Gina answers with a warm smile. She appears comfortable talking to Anna. I don't know who this is good for. Could all this talk about her substance abuse history trigger her to use drugs again?

"Tell me more about the family challenges," Anna encourages her. She places a clear clipboard on the table between the two of them.

"My husband Larry, I mean Laurence, was a school teacher here in Baltimore. He was such a great guy, he worked hard, was good with handling the bills, loved his sports, our daughter Tina, his mother and his sister Linda. When I couldn't steal enough from home to pawn and buy drugs, I stole from other family members, like my sister-in-law Linda, and her husband Cube. After the word got out about me to family and friends, I took advantage of the people in my church. When that song-and-game got old, I found a more effective way to make money. Prostitution. It started out harmlessly. I do a little something for someone, make a little money, then I get a hit. After a while, my addiction became more important than eating, my daughter or my husband. Larry caught me once with a drug dealer in the house. I worked off a debt with the drug dealer using sex in exchange. He and his friends assaulted Larry afterward. They also robbed the house. There was nothing Larry could say to me, I knew it was time for me to go. I had put him and Tina, our daughter, in danger. I left. From that moment on, I was a sex worker in Ridgely Square. I refused to go home out of fear I would put my family in danger again."

"Where is your husband Larry now, has he forgiven you?" Anna asks, never breaking eye contact.

"Larry died in a robbery while leaving from his job. If I'm completely honest with you, I may know something about who did it. I owed this guy some money, he didn't want me to touch him, he didn't want to beat me up, so he gave me two options: I give him money or he was going to kill me. I told him that my husband was a school teacher, and he may have money on him. If the guy had told my husband the money was for me, Larry would have given him the money. Instead, the guy attempted to rob my husband and killed him. He never got a dime from Larry."

"Did you tell the police?" Anna asks. She notices Gina reaching for the box of tissues and wiping her eyes.

"I did. After I learned of Larry's death, I went to the police station and I told them who did it. At first, the police brushed me off, then they picked the guy up. I was never charged with anything. I wish I was. I chose not to go to Larry's funeral because I felt like his death was my fault. Eventually, my usage stopped being just addiction and became compounded with me trying to kill myself for causing my husband's murder. It was like God was punishing me for surviving and abandoning my family. Then I met someone who was like a daughter to me."

"Silk?" Anna asks, leaning back in her chair.

"Yes, Silk Diamond. Silk was a transwoman. She was born Simon Little, the son of Sedrick and Erica Little. Two very wealthy people that have aligned themselves with Titan Industries with the goal of reconstructing the Ridgely Square community. They basically distanced themselves from Simon as he went through his transformation and became Silk. Silk then did well for herself, worked as a radio personality, then lost her job and her home. She faced difficulties finding employment as a transgender who was blackballed from the entertainment industry here in Baltimore. She started sex working in the area I used to work in. I kinda took her under my wing and saw her as my daughter. One day she was killed by one of her johns, another name for a customer, for those that don't know the jargon. It was in that moment I realized I was killing myself, and I had a daughter of my own who needed me. Death is definitive. You can't get the time back you missed. So I made it a point to reconnect with my daughter and my family. But first I had to get clean. So I went into treatment."

Noticing that Gina has been crying nonstop, I wonder why Anna hasn't paused the interview. I feel like it is cruel to have Gina go through all of this without taking a breather.

"After I got out of treatment, I attempted to reconnect with my daughter Tina. I learned from a newspaper that she committed suicide. I then tried to reconnect with my surviving family members, only to learn that my family was in shambles. The matriarch, Larry's mother died, my niece Kenya died, my sister-in-law was moving to another state and her husband Cube raped my daughter and is on the run. The only person I had to bond with was Linda and Cube's daughter Tiffany. The same person I stole so many items from when she was a little girl. I stole her television and Nintendo. Tiffany also witnessed me stealing money, silverware, and jewelry from her grandmother, Florence Simms. I truly thank God every day that she has attempted to give me a second chance."

"It's not like I really want to," I say, under my breath, rolling my eyes. But to be honest, Gina's words are tugging at my heart. It hurts to hear how messed up Gina was.

"Would you like to take a break?" Anna finally asks my aunt.

"No, let's keep going. I learned that my daughter liked the boy, Tyrone Clinton, who was shot and killed by the police for robbing a carryout back in December. Funny story and I can prove it: after the deaths of Tyrone and Kennard, there were riots that happened throughout Baltimore City. The Alphas took over as one of the dominant gangs in Ridgely Square when Sergeant Bell, one of the commanding officers of the Narcotics and Firearms Task Force brought several bags of prescription pills to the leader of the Alphas in exchange for a large sum of money."

"Excuse me?" Anna asks, leaning completely forward in her chair. I'm still not sure what I just heard my aunt say.

"I recorded the whole thing on my phone. Bell and his team from NAFA went into the pharmacies during the riots and they got all the prescription drugs, and they sold them to the Alphas. How many times have you been to a pharmacy, Anna? Do you know how long it takes the people that work there to get your medication? They have to locate the key and get the medication from the area. The people rioting were in and out in about 60 seconds tops. There was smoke and fire in a lot of those stores. Who could have easily slipped in and out of the stores and knew where to get the controlled drugs? I can tell you who did because I have access to the video footage of the evidence."

"Stop recording!" Ms. Clair yells as she walks to the sound stage. She is a brown-skinned, silver-and-black-haired, thin-framed woman. She does not look happy, but damn those heels she's wearing are vicious. "Thank you so much for everything, Gina, but please give Anna and me one minute to talk about this."

"What's wrong?" Anna asks, confused as to why Ms. Clair stopped the recording of her documentary. Several other people from the studio huddle around Ms. Clair and Anna as I walk close to the sound stage that Gina is sitting at, wiping tears from her face and blowing her nose.

"Do you understand the challenges of airing this documentary with the accusations that this woman is making?" Ms. Clair asks Anna.

"I am completely aware, as you do know my legal background," Anna responds boldly. "Gina says she has proof. I say let's record it. She has been very honest about everything so far."

"Gina, do you have any real proof backing the statements you made about the police officers you mentioned?" Ms. Clair asks, watching as Gina pulls out her cell phone and goes through several videos and hands the phone to Ms. Clair and Anna. Ms. Clair, Anna, and several stage people watch the video in silence and then rewatch it a couple more times.

"Has anyone else ever seen this?" Anna asks Gina with a look of concern on her face.

"No, I couldn't trust anybody with this aside from my niece, Tiffany who's standing right here," Gina answers, as she points my way. "I have no real family, aside from my niece."

"Before we get back to recording, what was in the other bags that the Alphas gave Bell and the other officers?" Ms. Clair asks very hesitantly.

"They gave Bell cash and gift cards. A lot of Bell's people used gift cards for purchases," Gina answers showing Ms. Clair more videos of Bell looking at gift cards and cash in the black trash bags he received from NAFA.

A short Asian woman that appears to be in her early twenties with pink hair approaches Ms. Clair looking at a tablet says, "Ms. Clair you have a Bishop Stokes that would like to see you."

"Thank you, Jewel, please tell her I will need to reschedule," Ms. Clair responds.

"I don't know if you should talk about this," I plead with my aunt. "These are cops, and you are about to play with their money. Leave the gangs and the cops alone."

"Somebody has to take down this group of bad cops," Anna interjects. "These are bad apples. I am very pro-cop, but I am strongly against bad apples. The growing number of murders in the city stem from something, and the drugs have become a common theme in a lot of these deaths. The Alphas have become the most dominant gang in Baltimore City, not just Ridgely Square. If we can remove the crooked cops from NAFA and shut down the activity with the gangs, maybe we can get things to go back to normal. And guess who would get credit for all of this being set in motion? You, Ms. Clair and the network."

"Why does it have to be you?" I ask my aunt, hoping that she can give me a reason. I am legit fearful for a woman I barely can stand. Is this love? Do I still love my aunt? Well, family is family. My father was a rapist and my mother was an enabler. How is loving them any different from loving a recovering manipulative drug addict? I love her. If love can keep her alive, love is what I will give her.

"I have to do this. Someone has to bring down NAFA; it's the least I can do after all the hurt I've caused. Maybe I can do some good," Gina responds. I know she is right.

"Actually, I need you all to bring in Sasha, Tyrone Clinton's mother as well. I have someone else that has been trying to go on air to speak about NAFA, but he will only do so if he can speak with Sasha on-air tomorrow."

"No!" I yell in anger in Anna's face. Oh my god, I'm yelling in Anna-freaking-Cartwright's face! This woman has been a prime-time icon for years, and I just stood up to this woman. "She's in no shape to come in. Her son was murdered last year."

"Tiffany, I can sense you have a protector's spirit, and I love it, but it is important that your friend Sasha comes in tomorrow for an interview if we are going to proceed with your aunt's interview. Especially with these developments about NAFA. I have been holding something of value for a few days, and I had nothing to back it up. Your aunt just provided me the proof I need."

I look away and notice a familiar face in the distance. No one can see her; she strongly favors me, but she's younger. It's my cousin Tina. The last time I saw her was the day my youngest daughter died in the car accident, but I see her clear as day. She shakes her head in agreement, almost appearing to tell me that I should agree with Anna Cartwright. I know she isn't real, but she looks so real. At that very moment, she vanished. That's weird. Have I always seen stuff that wasn't there or did this just start?

"Fine, but I'm coming too," I tell Anna. I know for sure this is going to end badly. I don't want this on my soul. I hope Sasha or Hakeem helped the kids with their homework.

Chapter 5

The next day after I got off work from the hospital, I walked to the community center to check on Hakeem. He sometimes becomes too buried in his job. The air is a little chilly, but springtime in Baltimore is very inconsistent. As I walk through the glass door of the community center and towards the classroom area, I notice Hakeem and his brother Jamar are meeting. Hakeem invited me into the conversation.

"Tiffany, let me ask you, if you had the means to fight back against Titan, would you?" Jamar asks beating Hakeem to whatever statement was on the tip of his tongue.

"It depends on what you mean by fight back. If you mean legally, yes. If you mean bombing Chandler and Chanel Titan, along with Sedrick and Erica Little, no," I answer. Chandler and Chanel Titan are siblings and real estate icons in the United States. They have invested a lot of money and time trying to reinvent the Ridgely Square community into something different. They partnered with Sedrick and Erica Little, a husband and wife team who were both born into wealth as their parents own an airline company and a luxurious hotel chain.

"My idea is legal, but it requires strategy," Jamar says, leaning forward and looking me in the eye. "We have money, Hakeem and his church friends have money. We go into partnership, we purchase all of the homes in Ridgely Square that are in default on their taxes or about to be taken by the banks, and we turn this community 100% black. The moment we control our property, we control what happens with our schools, with what stores and food we want sold in our community, and we have a stronger say so with the police department. I do not see what is so hard to understand."

"It's because you're trying to make it about race," Hakeem answers.

"What's the problem with that, Hakeem?" Jamar snarls back. "Redlining was about race. Do you know where that housing discrimination started? Here in Baltimore. Economic inequality has a racial component, health options have a racial component, everything in our day-to-day lives has a racial divide, but the second we try to challenge it, it's about race? Are you hearing yourself? My brother, you have to pick a lane. You can't ask for justice for all but get scared when you have the chance to make justice for yourself."

"Did you watch my aunt's interview last night?" I ask. Hakeem breaks his stare from his brother and gazes in my direction.

"I did," Jamar answers. "The whole city has been talking about the part that led to Ms. Clair screaming, 'Stop the cameras.' Did your aunt really have proof that the police were selling drugs and working with the Alphas?"

"She does. For that reason alone, I actually agree with what you said before; we need our own police for the community," I respond. Hakeem rests back in his chair, silent and appearing disgusted by my statement.

"What's wrong with you?" Jamar asks Hakeem, noticing the visible anger on his face. I can't help but wonder what is wrong with Hakeem myself.

Hakeem answers, "Tiffany, your safety is what's wrong. Your aunt is about to go at it with a protected gang—the police. Your aunt isn't just talking about a couple of Alphas, Cabal members or Crips, or Bloods, she's talking about a special force unit of officers who also work with the Alphas. Have you not seen what happens to witnesses in court cases? Their homes are firebombed, they get killed on the way to work. They don't value life. The only decent cop we had in this community was Officer Carter, and he was killed at the hospital the day Kennard was shot."

"He was killed by people that identified themselves as protesters from your group, Justice for All," Jamar adds. Hakeem moved his head to the side, in an almost challenging motion to Jamar before looking back at me. "Your aunt Gina is with you all the time, which could make you a target. You have children, which makes them a target. Sasha, whose son was killed by Officers Lake and Moreland, also becomes a target in this again. Your aunt's new friend, Anna Cartwright attacked Sasha in the media and blamed her for Tyrone's involvement in the convenience store robbery. When we tried to investigate why he was shot after he surrendered to the police, the whole police department came down on Sasha. Are you sure you want to be associated with this?"

I don't know how to answer Hakeem, and he's right. I honestly don't want to be a part of this. I wish Gina would have kept her big mouth closed. While in thought I notice Tina standing behind Hakeem, again nodding in agreement, she has a warm smile. Wait, can I see ghosts now? As much as I loved my cousin, I would rather see my daughter Kenya. As what appeared to be my cousin Tina vanishes, I can hear my daughter Kenya whisper, "You're doing the right thing, Mom," in my ear. I notice that no one is aware of the events that just transpired. I stand up and I leave the classroom without answering Jamar or Hakeem. The two begin to argue among themselves as I walk out of the community center.

While walking up the sidewalk I keep noticing everyone that walks in my eye view has Tina's or Kenya's face. I also hear the word "mom" repeating constantly in my head. The voice is undeniably Kenya's. As my heart rate increases and I can feel the weight of my breath get lighter entering and leaving my body, a skinny light-skinned male with a short haircut approaches me.

"Hey ma," the boy says, wearing a zipped-down hoodie with a black t-shirt underneath. "Why you look so stressed out, beautiful?"

I hear him as background noise, but I keep hearing Kenya's voice clearly. I'm having a hard time pulling it together. Maybe my lack of sleep is catching up with me. "I'm sorry, who are you?"

"They call me Milk," the young man says. He looks like he should be in high school, probably no older than 17 years old. What should be the sclera of his eyes are a dark yellow, and his lips are a dark brown. "What you doing out here?"

"None of your business," I answer. He places his hand on my arm, preventing me from walking away.

"Let me help you, beautiful. Let me pay your rent or something," he asks, gripping my arm tighter and pulling me towards him.

"No, get off me."

"Let me help you with your kids then."

"What did you just say?"

"You got four kids, they come this way every day to go to school. Let me help you with them."

"No, and stay the hell away from my children."

"Can't do that. I own this block right here. From here on out, it's a sidewalk tax. You got to do something for me in order to get through."

I keep trying to break his grip, but this little guy is strong. "I don't have to do anything, weirdo."

"Technically, you don't have to do anything. Let me and some of my brothers stash in your yard or in your house and we cool."

"Hell no," I reply. The idea of hiding drugs in my house or my yard is absurd. I don't know who this little bastard thinks he is, but there is no way in hell I'm hiding his drugs in my house or on my property.

"I'm not asking you, I'm telling you," Milk says as he notices Hakeem walking in my direction. "You know I'm an Alpha. You know what the other option is."

Milk breaks his grip and walks towards Hakeem, makes brief eye contact with Hakeem and then continues to walk up the street. Amazingly, my hallucinations stop, but I have a whole new concern: The Alphas know about my children and where I live. I shouldn't be helping with Gina and this interview stuff.

Chapter 6

Inside the Nubian studio, there are six seats set up in the area where Anna Cartwright is sitting. The table has been removed from the center, and Gina is sitting next to Sasha. I could not convince Sasha not to do this interview. I'm on edge a little because, well who wants to go to war with the police? My boyfriend Hakeem and Sasha technically did last year. It was because of the two police officers that shot and killed her son who was involved in the robbery of a carryout.

Anna Cartwright leans back for a moment, sitting upright as the cameras begin to film. "Welcome to the latest installment of our documentary, Baltimore: A City on Fire. I'm your host Anna Cartwright, and I'm joined by my guests Gina Simms and Sasha Greene. Sasha is the mother of the late Tyrone Clinton, who was shot and killed by police in the 2016 robbery of a carryout in the Ridgely Square community. The robbery led to a series of riots, another child's death at the hands of police, more riots and the death of police officer, Edward Carter. Sasha, welcome to the show."

"Thank you, Anna," Sasha says, looking around the studio, making very little eye contact with me, and then turning her attention back to Anna. Sasha has dressed appropriately today but faintly smells like she woke up in the middle of a barfight. It took a lot of effort to get her to come to the studio without drinking. Sasha's hand tremors uncontrollably. I'm not sure if she's nervous or if she needs a drink.

"Sasha, can you please tell us about your son, Tyrone, along with any challenges you have gone through over the last few months,"

Anna asks as Gina gently grabs hold of Sasha's right hand. She holds it in warm support. I wonder why Anna is so concerned with Sasha's story now. A few months ago, Anna blamed Sasha's son for the death of the store owner and commended the police officers for the murder of Tyrone.

"Well, my son was a good kid. He loved football, he was a running back for his high school. His coach was actually the police officer that was killed, Edward Carter. Officer Carter, we called him Coach Eddie, was going to let my son use his car to go to the prom. I worked at the hospital, and received government assistance, so I didn't make a lot of money. I told Tyrone that he wasn't going to be able to go to the prom, even with the car that Coach Eddie was going to provide; I didn't have enough to pay for the tuxedo. My son really wanted to go to prom with this girl he'd had a crush on for a while. Her name was Tina Simms. It's a small world; I didn't know until recently that Tina was Gina's daughter."

"It *is* a small world," Anna interjects as Gina and Sasha smile.

"Since the death of my son, the apartment that I lived in changed ownership to Titan Industries, they displaced all of us and then demolished the building. Titan Industries provided a lot of residents a voucher to move to Baltimore County. My son was a senior at his high school, so I didn't want to move to the county when he was going to graduate in a few months, so I refused the voucher for Baltimore County. Myself and several others were displaced and Titan placed all of our items on the street without a warning. The courts ruled it as an eviction and because it was ruled as an eviction I lost the voucher I had for Baltimore City. Titan only provided us with 12 days to relocate, along with moving out our belongings. Sometimes the moving process with our vouchers can take 60 to 90 days. Tiffany was nice enough to allow me to move into the home that she inherited from her grandmother. I often feel like I'm a burden because I'm not supposed to be there."

I'm completely shocked by the statements Sasha makes. I have never, nor would I ever make Sasha feel like she is not welcome in my home. She was never a burden and I wonder where that thought came from.

"I grew up in the Ridgely Square community," Sasha continues, looking down at the floor. "I grew up poor, my daddy sold drugs and lived in several different houses. My momma and I lived in the old high rises. I met my son's father, Paris, when I was a in high school. Paris made a lot of money selling crack. He had the nicest cars and owned a home. I saw a life with him I would never have in a thousand lifetimes. We took trips to the beach, we ate at nice restaurants, we went to casinos, we stayed in the best hotels, and we saw boxing matches. We did all the stuff that I never did in my life. We had a son, it was beautiful. Then one day, he got locked up and everything was taken away from me. The money, the house, all I had was my son, and we lived in a shelter until we got a voucher."

"You do realize that your boyfriend, Paris Clinton took the lives of two people?" Anna asks in a condescending tone. Anna's facial expression changes; she appears annoyed with Sasha. Oh yeah, she is a prosecutor, of course she would get angry at the thought of a drug dealing murderer.

"I did, but Paris was also a father," Sasha rebuts. "He taught Tyrone how to count, how to read, how to ride a bicycle, and he helped with the homework. Tyrone was reading at a 7th grade level when he was in 2nd grade, all because of his father. I know that because Paris was incarcerated when Tyrone was in 2nd grade. But you're right, Paris broke the law, and he is in prison now because of the choices he made. After we received the voucher, I had new goals: to help my son graduate high school, go to college, and not become a statistic. I also wanted to get off of government assistance and go to college. But as they say, if you ever want to make God laugh, tell Him your plan."

Tears begin to fall from Sasha's eyes again. Anna's facial expression changes to concern as two of the audiovisual technicians provide me with a small black box they place on the side of my jeans and a tiny microphone they ask me to run under my shirt. I am told to join Sasha on stage as support. This is completely unexpected. I do not want to be on camera. I don't even want to be here.

"The day I lost my son, I felt an emptiness, like the world was moving in slow motion. I thought about all my regrets, like telling Tyrone he wouldn't be able to go to his prom. He was so happy that Coach Eddie was going to let him drive that car. I just can't believe Tyrone is gone. I couldn't see my son for several days after they killed him. The police kept telling me he was evidence. A beautiful baby boy I brought home from the hospital was murdered and I couldn't see him."

"At least you were there for your son every day," Gina interjects. "My daughter, who was going to prom with your son, was raised between her father and my mother-in-law. I was so busy trying to chase a high, I missed every moment in her life. Tina was in love with the Williams sisters, but I never got a chance to take her to any of their tennis matches. You were a good mother that made every sacrifice to save her son from the evils of the world. I was a selfish piece of garbage that allowed the evils of the world to find my daughter."

"Uncle Larry took Tina to see the Williams sister play tennis at the U.S. Open or the French Open. I forget which one," I respond under my breath.

"At least you don't have to tell your daughter's father," Sasha rebuts with a sad chuckle. "Paris writes to me every week, sometimes two times. He asks me to visit him, give him my phone number, anything. I do nothing. Not because I don't want to see him, but how do I tell the father of our child I failed our child? I guess I would tell him something if I knew something. The only thing I have is the video and a police report."

Anna leans back in her chair, looking at an empty chair next to her, then looks back at Gina and Sasha with a serious expression on her face. "I hope today can resolve some of those feelings and provide more answers. For some time I have had a person wanting to speak to you about your son's murder, Ms. Greene. I would like to introduce him to you."

A skinny, very young-looking white male walks to the sound stage and sits next to Anna. His dark brown hair is combed back and has a lot of stubble. "Hi Ms. Sasha Greene, I can't tell you how sorry I am. My name is Eric Moreland; I'm one of the responding officers that met with your son the day he was killed."

"You are one sick person, bringing her son's murderer to this interview!" I yell at Anna as some of the stage crew walk towards the stage. I get so overcome with anger I attempt to punch her, but Anna does not flinch.

"No, Tiffany, please listen to what he has to say," Anna responds and Sasha sobs uncontrollably.

"I had no intention for what happened to take place. I had to make a split-second decision. I heard the word gun from my partner, Officer Lake, and he drew his weapon and started shooting. Moments before that we heard the shot fired in the store that killed the owner. I believe your son was a good kid. That event has haunted me since it happened. I love kids, I saw innocence and fear in his eyes when my partner began shooting."

"Please stop talking," Sasha mutters while sobbing.

An awkward silence fills the room, and I am tempted to punch Officer Moreland. I look at my aunt, who is hugging Sasha, then I look back at Anna. Why did we put ourselves up for this? Why did she bring us here? Why is she doing this? "What is the point of this," I say, breaking the silence.

"I have been living with tremendous guilt since what happened to Tyrone," Officer Moreland responds. "After being placed on administrative leave, I was placed on the Narcotics and Firearms Task Force. I went from making a horrible decision to working with a bunch of drug dealers acting like the police. I have attempted to come out with this information for several months, but Anna kept telling me that they could not do anything with my story. Then when you all began to talk about NAFA, I had to help. Sasha, I'm so sorry for what I've done, but please let me help stop NAFA from destroying any more lives."

Officer Moreland is also crying, I feel that he is telling the truth about his feelings. There is something trustworthy about his facial expressions. Sasha is still silent, so I decide to speak up for her. "I knew Tyrone, he was a good kid. He lived on a different floor in my apartment building. He helped with the groceries, he came home with his lacrosse and football uniform on every day after practice, and played catch with my kids on the sidewalk some nights. You and your partner didn't just kill her son, you took the life of a person from this community. A person that didn't sell drugs, a person that deserved a second chance. Do you understand that?"

"That is something I truly understand," Officer Moreland answers with tears streaming from his eyes. "I would have loved to see that kid play college football or become a community leader. I heard gunshots and I was scared. I can't stress enough how sorry I am. If I can help in any way with taking down Bell and the others in NAFA, I will help. Again, Ms. Sasha Greene, I am so sorry."

"What did my son take?" Sasha asks with an angry tone. Since December, Sasha had hoped to learn anything about her son's death. The look on her face is so grim, so empty, and emotionless.

Officer Moreland takes a deep breath, looks at Sasha and me then looks down at the empty space between us before responding. "He didn't have anything in his pocket except for the keys to his apartment and the phone number of a young lady named Tina. We searched his locker at school and found an autographed picture of Serena and Venus Williams. The toxicology report came back, and he was squeaky clean. Derrick, the young man that we arrested did everything, including stealing the money out of the register. After watching the cameras, we learned that he also bullied Tyrone throughout the robbery. I have no idea why your son was with him, ma'am, but it appears that your son did not want to be there. I am so sorry that he's not here to tell his side of the story."

The awkward silence returns and I feel a pain in my stomach. I hear Sasha say something very low under her breath before she looks up with perfect posture, making eye contact with Officer Moreland. "Go to hell," Sasha says before walking off the sound stage.

Chapter 7

Sitting at the round wooden table inside the kitchen, my daughter Desha hands me her math homework. Desha is tall for her age and a little pudgy. She has her hair in a long ponytail, with a white shirt that has dirt and stains from food on it. "I hate fractions," she says as I read through her work. She has almost every answer right.

"You may hate something, but you still give it the same effort you would something you love," I respond out of instinct. I have heard Hakeem preach that in his sermons several times. I have not spoken to him since before the interview with Anna, earlier today. I'm almost positive he watched the show and will have a lot to say about Officer Moreland speaking with Sasha. All things considered, Sasha handled herself well.

"Can I go to bed now, please?" Desha asks, rolling her eyes at me.

I notice a piece of paper on the floor near the refrigerator; as I turn it around I realize that it's a picture of Kenya. Desha glances at the picture and then storms off to her bedroom. What was that about? Before I can comment on Desha's actions, RJ walks by me with his pants soaking wet. "What is wrong with you, boy, why didn't you piss in the toilet?" I ask as he shrugs his shoulders. I grab RJ by his arm and we walk to the bathroom, where I begin to run water in the tub. RJ is too old to be pissing on himself.

"Can I help?" Sasha asks, walking into the bathroom as I hold RJ's arm. She looks very relaxed and does not smell like alcohol. I don't smell cigarette smoke either.

"RJ can wash himself, but can you talk to Desha for me? I think she's upset with me," I ask as RJ pulls away from me to take off his clothes in his bedroom. I then go down to the basement for a moment of silence before I call it a night. Hopefully I can go to sleep and stay asleep for a full night. As I sit on a wooden chair with a brown cushion, I notice a clock that reads 12:34. I enjoy the silence briefly before hearing a male's voice.

"How does it feel to take handouts from that woman who wouldn't let me into her house?" the masculine voice asks. I look around and realize the voice is my father's. Well, not really his but a voice that has been in my head for a while. But it sounds really real. His voice and my mother's voice often keep me up at night, making it hard to sleep or stay asleep.

"It's not a handout, Daryl," another deeper, sharper voice says. A voice that I instantly remember. My grandmother, Florence Simms. She died last year and left me this house. She never got along with my father. She and my uncle Larry, Gina's husband were my biggest advocates and defenders from my dysfunctional parents.

"Daryl, you think because a house has been in a family for generations, it is a handout," my grandmother retorts. "The fact of the matter is, having something worth leaving to your children and grandchildren is the best way to amass wealth. Look at you, what did you accomplish? You are a very good mechanic, several convictions, known child molester and own nothing. You lived in my daughter's rental property, but if you were worth a damn, I would have allowed you to live here."

"Liar, you hated me," my father rebuts. "You wanted me to fail. You wanted Tiffany to fail. You laughed at her for her several children."

"You fool," she interjects. "Her behavior was because of your behavior. Your destruction cost her a decent youth. Do you have any idea how many nights she would sneak and call me crying because she couldn't sleep? Having nightmares you were coming into her room. She feared you being there when she came home from school. It's amazing she finished high school and is in college. You didn't help and my daughter Linda didn't do a damn thing to help."

"So you want to take credit for everything she has done right?" my father asks as I wonder how much time has passed.

"No, Tiffany did this on her own. But to be honest, Larry did help a lot with her success in high school and early on in college. But Tiffany did all the work. Daryl, Tiffany is a part of this family's legacy. I left her this house as an investment in our future. She is raising the kids on her own. You left her nothing before you jumped bail and went on the run. You invested nothing but trauma in her life while I was alive. Your behavior led to the death of my other granddaughter Tina. Your shadow over her life is so big that even now you are hunting her as a figment of her imagination."

"Tiffany never went hungry nor did she have bad grades. Do you have your head so far up your own ass you only see the bad in what I did? Do you think I just tormented her throughout her life? Who put up the ceiling fans in your house? Me! Who painted your house?

Me! Who fixed Larry's car? Me! You look down on me for a mistake, but that mistake doesn't take away from all the good I did."

"You got sexual pleasure from underaged girls, you pervert," my grandmother responds with a sharp tone.

"You act like what I did haunted her every day. Like every single day. She got over it. Look at her. She's in school, working at the hospital and never was arrested. So obviously what I did wasn't that bad."

"And here you are, haunting her right now," my grandmother says.

"And what are you doing?" my father questions my grandmother.

"In life as in death, her guardian angel," my grandmother answers. In that moment everything in the basement grows quiet and I notice the clock shows 12:34 a.m.

Chapter 8

Inside the Allen Bradley Funeral Home, I sit in a circle with other women for our weekly grief and loss group. I feel better about sharing today, but I still hold back information because, well, telling a bunch of strangers that your dead grandmother is having conversations with your living father that molested you growing up sounds a bit out there. Also the arguments only happen in the basement of the house because your father is on the run from the police. Never mind, I get that it sounds crazy.

Today's subject is *Words Never Said.* I take a deep breath before speaking. I'm nervous. I couldn't care less about Gina's and Sasha's thoughts, but these strangers, these grieving women that are mourning and really have problems. I don't want them to think less of me. I exhale and let the words come out.

"I'm not home enough. I have four surviving children, and I spend more time between work, school, and community projects than I do at home. When I am home, reality just weighs on me. When I was at the apartment, I put Keyon, my ex-boyfriend out the house. I was proud of him after he finally got his life together. He got a good job in HVAC and took good care of our daughter, Kenya. I wish I could tell him that he was a great father, a great friend, and I wish we could have worked things out."

I look down and notice a stain on my blue jeans when I hear Gina's voice. "I'm so sorry," she says, looking in my direction. "Tiffany, you were my favorite niece, and at times I thought of you as my second daughter. You were better to my actual daughter Tina than I was to her at times."

Gina then adjusted how she was seated, leaning to her right side and resting her elbow on her leg. "It was a cold day in Baltimore when Larry, my deceased husband and I brought Tina home from the hospital after she was born. Tina was a happy baby, she had great sleeping habits, she ate everything I cooked, she had a beautiful smile, and as she grew she developed a love for singing and tennis. She and Larry used to love watching tennis, baseball, and basketball together. When my addiction got out of hand, I left. I knew I was a cancer to the family. Of course my actions led to Larry being killed in a robbery, and if I was an actual mother, Tina would still be alive. So I really wish I could say the words, I'm sorry to Larry and Tina."

"I would like to say I'm sorry to my two children," a small framed, light-skinned woman, possibly in her early 20s says. Her arms and neck are covered in tattoos, her hair is braided and dyed blue. Her eyes are a beautiful brown color, and she has an accent, she's not from Baltimore or the south, I cannot pick up on the accent. "My first child was murdered before he was 1 year old, my second was taken from me, and I don't know where she is."

"What is your name, sweetheart?" Ms. Toya asks with a warm voice. I knew I wasn't crazy. None of us have seen this woman before.

"If I tell you, do you promise not to tell anyone I was here?" the young woman asks nervously.

"Do you plan on hurting yourself or anyone else?" Ms. Toya responds with a question of her own with a gentle smile still resting on her face.

"No, I don't want to hurt anyone or myself. I just went through so much, and I don't know who to trust. I saw those two women walk in here, and I felt this was a safe place," the young woman says, pointing at Gina and me.

"You have nothing to worry about; everything said here is confidential," Ms. Toya answers as the young woman sighs.

"My name is Lela," the young woman states and leans back. "I'm originally from Seattle, Washington. This gang called the Alphas constantly moves me around. When I had my son, they killed him and moved me to Arizona, then Texas, then New Mexico, and a few other places. I was in San Francisco when I had my daughter. They separated me from her about a year ago, and have moved me around continually since then. I escaped from a motel a few days ago, but I'm fearful to return home to my parents. They say they will kill me and my parents."

I get a sick feeling in my stomach as she speaks, I'm fearful for this woman's life and for ours because she is here, seemingly on the run from the Alphas.

"I feel powerless because they have my daughter, and all I want is to get her back and go back to Seattle with my parents. Gina, I saw you doing the interviews, can you help me?" Lela asks, confirming that sick feeling was not in vain.

"This is not the place for that," Ms. Toya interjects. "I will allow a break for you two to discuss the challenges you are currently experiencing, Lela."

After the end of the group session, Gina wasted no time talking to her, and of course I agreed to provide support. Sometimes I feel my aunt will be the death of me. Seriously, she barely has a hand on the proverbial steering wheel of her own life and she's trying to impact someone else's. I can't be the only person that has noticed this, right?

Wasting no time with subtleties, Gina told Lela her history of sex work in the old market place area and her history of substance abuse when Lela stopped her.

"I was forced into this life." Lela exhales with panic. "My mother and I went shopping at a supermarket when I was kidnapped at gunpoint in the parking lot. My parents weren't special; my father worked at a fish market, my mother was a custodian at a middle school. They didn't take me for money. They had me staying in motels, they drugged me, forced me to have sex for money, then moved me to different places every so many months. They punished me every time I got pregnant from their customers. It got to the point I believed them when they told me my parents didn't love me. They brainwash you. Force you to think this is what love is. They tell you when to eat, sleep and how to dress. They rate you, and once your rating drops too low, they kill you because you no longer have value."

"Would you mind talking about this on air, so the world can know the kind of monsters that are out there preying on you?" Gina asks with no hesitation.

"What are you doing? She needs to be reunited with her parents. She needs protection," I answer quickly.

"Gina is right," Lela explains. She moves closer to us as she talks. Her eyes and facial expressions are very engaging. "I need to talk about this, I will never see my parents or my daughter again unless I shine a light on the Alphas and NAFA that works with the Alphas. The motel I was staying at has NAFA regularly checking in on the girls staying there."

"Where have you been staying?" I ask.

"The last few nights I stayed in the back of an abandoned truck parked in the rear of a dilapidated warehouse. It's the one that has a giant milk bottle on the front of the building," Lela answers, rubbing her shoulders.

"We can't have you staying there, that's the old Ridgley Dairy building. I used to take customers there. That place isn't the safest. Some of the Alphas stash bodies in there, or smoke weed in there, or cut school and just hang out in there. Basically, that is not a safe place," Gina quickly infers.

"We cannot bring her to my house," I tell Gina abruptly. "I have my kids and Sasha there. The last thing I need is for the Alphas or NAFA to show up at my house because of Gina's new pet project."

"I'm ok, I can find somewhere to stay," Lela responds gently, rubbing my hand. I back up, feeling uncomfortable.

"She can stay with me," Gina volunteers. I almost expected that answer.

Chapter 9

The sun is setting, and the children are in the front yard playing soccer as I walk to the steps and see Sasha drinking a bottle of beer. Two empty bottles are sitting upright on her left side. Before I can say anything to Sasha about drinking in front of the kids, I notice a Ziploc sandwich bag filled with pills near one of the bushes in front of my home. I pick up the bag filled with pills and ask Sasha, "Are these yours too?"

"I don't do no drugs, Tiffany, you know that. I don't know where they came from," Sasha answers, putting a cigarette in her mouth and lighting it. I throw the bag of pills in the street and then walk back to the house as I hear a male's voice yell at me.

"Put them back!" the voice yells repeatedly. I turn around and notice the voice came from Milk, one of my neighborhood's exclusive drug dealers.

"Get out of here, Milk. The kids are playing, nobody has time for your nonsense tonight," Sasha yells before inhaling her cigarette.

"I'm not talking to you, I'm talking to her. Pick them up and put them back where I had them," Milk demands.

"Excuse you," I answer. "This my house, you don't pay no bills here. Take your pills and all that somewhere else."

"Them pills are my money, pick up my money, and put them back where I had them. Unless you want me to body them dirty ass kids of yours," Milk demands.

"Who do you think you're talking to?" I say, walking towards Milk as a tall, brown-skinned, muscular man walks behind Milk and places a hand on his shoulder. The man has a close haircut with deep waves and is wearing black military-style pants, black boots, with a black shirt under a black bulletproof vest.

"Chill, Milk," the man says. I notice a police badge hanging from one of the chains around his neck, along with another chain with dog tags. "I'm so sorry about his behavior, Ms. Gibbons. My name is Sergeant Marshawn Bell, is it ok if we talk inside? I would love to talk to you in private. I come in peace."

Bell has a smile on his face and speaks in a soothing tone. He appears harmless and intimidating at the same time. I notice the handgun, the mace, the taser, and the handcuffs on his belt. Sasha frowns in disapproval as I walk towards the door and open it, inviting him inside. Bell and I walk to the kitchen area and sit down. I think to myself, What would my grandmother think, knowing I have a drug dealer threatening to keep drugs in her front yard and this police officer sitting at her table.

"I apologize about Milk's behavior," Bell begins, sitting back in the chair. He looks over at the pictures on the refrigerator, then back at me. A smile never leaves this young man's face. He is very attractive and toned. Could this be the same Bell that Gina talked about?

"Are you going to lock him up? He admitted to having drugs that he is trying to stash in my yard," I say as Bell laughs.

"You want to file a report on that, make yourself a target? These people burn down homes while families sleep. These are the same people that kill people who show up to court. Milk is a prominent member of the gang called the Alphas, and as hard as it is to admit, nowhere in this state is safe from that gang. They are in your kids' school, at your job, they are in your neighborhood. What do you want me to do, file a report? Ok, they'll send a message. You won't like the message."

I realize this is the Bell that Gina is talking about. He is very confident and very relaxed. He has a light-heartedness to him that is intriguing. "Why are you here, to threaten me?"

"No," Bell answers. "Your aunt had a lot to say about me on the broadcast. People have the right to their opinions. I'm fine with that. My mother raised me and my autistic brother by herself, basically. She was a school teacher until she had to resign because of a disability. My father, well my father was murdered. Now my mother, who has pancreatic cancer, needs me to help her and my special needs brother. I looked into cancer centers, a lot of the affordable ones with my salary and her income are horrible. So, I looked into different ways to provide for my mother. There's a medical center in Virginia that provides a treatment to increase the chances of her living longer. I'm doing this long enough to pay for her treatment there."

"Are you about to kill me?" I ask. "I don't want to beg for my life, but I have my kids outside, and I really don't want them to come into the kitchen and see my dead body." My heart is beating faster. Bell's level of calmness, his hands resting on the table and the smile on his face make me wonder when he will shoot me.

Bell chuckles, he has very nice dimples and gorgeous teeth. He has a strong jawline. He shakes his head "no" in response to my question and rests his hands into each other, locking his fingers in a very relaxed position. Bell glances around the kitchen then back to me, making very good eye contact, still with a charming smile on his face.

"I have no intention of harming you, Ms. Gibbons. My goal is to bring balance to Ridgley Square. Something your grandmother tried to do. Something Pastor Avery tried to do. I'm trying to do the same thing. Companies like Titan Industries only want to move our people out of the community and make it a place you or I could never afford. What if we controlled the power that this community possesses? Your grandmother left you this house, why give it up? You go to work and go to school, why stop? People in this community sell and buy drugs. Why can't all parties coexist? If we control the chaos, we reduce the chances of good people like you getting hurt and we corral the chaos in the right direction."

"What are you talking about?" I fearfully ask as he continues to lean back in his chair with a smile still on his face. Such a perfect freaking smile.

"People like Milk will always exist, the Alphas, the Cabal, this gang, that gang, there will always be a gang. The murders will always happen in this city. The politicians will always use the murder rate, education rate, and employment rate as methods to get votes, but it won't get better. Your grandmother died, and the vacant buildings from 10 years ago are still vacant. The homeless people that lived up the street still live there. Why not control the narrative? Create a place where the drug dealers and drug addicts can interact, and the innocent people are safe. Your kids, you, Sasha, whoever.

The people who deserve to get killed die, and the innocent people go home and go to sleep. I manage the game to make sure nobody gets out of line."

"Then why do people like Milk want to stash his drugs in my yard?"

"Every police officer doesn't buy into my ideology. You still have your beat cops, and patrol officers that see someone like Milk and think, I have to get this guy off the street. They don't realize another Milk will have his spot before this Milk is placed in a holding cell. Why waste your tax dollars on locking up people that will be in and out of prison for selling the same drugs before they die from an overdose or are killed by the next drug dealer."

"Is that what you think?" I ask, leaning forward as Bell's eyes light up with excitement.

"That's what I know. We have over 300 murders a year, and they are typically carried out by the same group of people, year in and year out. I provide a suggestion, let the kids eat cake until all their teeth rot. We control them and we tax them. Las Vegas realized if you tax prostitutes, everybody would be happy. I realized if I tax the drug dealers, good people go to sleep at night."

"Why are you telling me all this?" I ask.

"Because I want you to realize, your aunt is attacking me for doing the right thing. We can lock up all the drug dealers and killers and someone will always take their place. I can tax the drug dealers and tell them where to sell, nobody outside of the drug game gets hurt. On top of that, I can get my mother to get the right kind of help with the money. If you let Milk and other dealers stash in your yard, other cops with different ideologies will get off their backs and we can all live happily together."

"Find another yard. By your own logic, if I let them stash in my yard, I become a part of the drug game. I would like to respectfully decline," I counter with fear in my heart. Bell is still relaxed and smiling. I can smell the fragrance of his cologne, it smells great.

"I can protect your children, Tiffany."

"Why couldn't you protect my daughter, or her father, or Tyrone Clinton or Kennard Lyles-Bey?" I ask as Bell stands up, then places the chair under the table. Bell then walks around the kitchen taking a closer look at the pictures on the refrigerator and he glances at the dish rack. Why didn't I put the dishes in the cabinet? There aren't enough hours in a day for all I have to do.

"I would love to give you the answer you want to hear, especially for your daughter, but I am an honest man. Some things are out of my control. For years people have played by the game of right and wrong, and people like Tyrone Clinton and Kennard Lyles-Bey were murdered. I prefer to offer something more balanced, and all I ask is for your support. Have a great night, Ms. Gibbons. No harm will come to you or your family tonight, you have my word. Do not worry about Milk trying to stash his drugs in your yard anymore. Your kids deserve somewhere safe to play. But it will come at a price, Ms. Gibbons. You will pay me $500 a week to ensure your children's safety from the Alphas." Bell's face takes on a stern look, then a bright smile before walking out of the kitchen area and to the front door.

Chapter 10

It's a grey morning in Baltimore, an overcast fills the sky and the streets are eerily empty today. I find myself at the community resource center with Hakeem and Jamar sitting inside of the boardroom at a grand wooden table. There is already strong tension between Jamar and Hakeem; I really wish they could bury the hatchet that separates them. We all have the same goal, but for some reason, Hakeem and Jamar have different views on how to achieve it.

"Yesterday I was approached by Milk from the Alphas. He was attempting to hide pills in my yard in broad daylight. My kids were in the yard playing," I say, annoyed with the thought of such an arrogant move.

"They have tried this before," Jamar chimes in. His face has a scowl, and he looks vexed. "They killed a friend of mine, Rubin. Rubin used to drive the bus, and he had twin daughters. He asked Milk and the Alphas to stop hiding drugs in his yard. Milk first threatened him, shot a hole in his car door, broke a window in his home, then placed bags of pills in visible areas where Rubin could find them, and Milk watched his reaction. One day Milk fired a gun at Rubin's feet, missing him by inches, and told him to 'stop acting soft.' Rubin called the police, and they locked up Milk. Rubin was murdered two days before the court date at his home by one of the Alphas. As a result, Milk's charges were dropped."

"Jesus, when did this happen?" Hakeem asks with concern.

"Last year. The murder and court case kind of got lost in the news due to the death of Tyrone Clinton," Jamar responds, looking down.

"Bell came to my house as well. He gave me a proposition, to hide the drugs in my yard for the Alphas. I said no. He then started talking about his mother and told me no harm would come to me if I paid him $500 a week," I tell Jamar and Hakeem.

"What did he tell you about his mother?" Hakeem asks, I notice the anger in his voice.

"She has pancreatic cancer, and he is trying to get her into some medical center in Virginia," I answer as Hakeem and Jamar look at each other. This is the first glance I have seen the two of them share without anger or animosity.

"This is why I keep saying we need our own police force; we can reduce the chances of this happening in our own community if we control the police force," Jamar interjects with anger.

"You do know Bell is black, right?" Hakeem questions.

"He is, but if we had our own medical centers, our own police, and owned all the homes in Ridgely Square, we would reduce the number of drug dealers, murderers, and people like Bell who would exploit our challenges," Jamar rebuts.

"I disagree, this would have happened regardless. The man's mother is dying and he is trying to save her. I don't agree with his method, but I completely understand. If he didn't have the job he has now, she might have already died. But if he were rich, she would have already been to Virginia and gotten the medical treatment," I state as Jamar and Hakeem look at me with confusion.

"What are you saying?" Hakeem asks.

"My grandmother died last year from Alzheimer's disease. She did more for me than my own parents. If I had the money to extend her life, I would have. My kids and I live in the house she left for me now. I would trade this house in a heartbeat to have her alive right now. Same with my daughter, Kenya. If I could get the money to keep her alive from selling or hiding Milk's drugs, you think I wouldn't? Let's be realistic while we try to plan for a better world. We all have a line we would cross if we could create a better world for our families. It doesn't make it right, but I totally understand."

"Then we need to learn how to control the line," Jamar quips. "We need to purchase every vacant lot and home in Ridgely Square. If we own the homes and stores we have the power. We control the tax dollars and the city will have to answer to us. We can have our own police force that we dictate what we need to be enforced."

"What about the Alphas and the drugs? How do we control that, do you plan on locking them up? Do they go through the regular court systems? What about people like Milk, who have no problem with murder? What will your police force do to them?" Hakeem asks.

"We educate and we rehabilitate. People like Milk are a product of the broken system, we are trying to create a better system. We can create that system and Milk can be fixed," Jamar answers. Hakeem rolls his eyes. The animosity between the two begins to rise again.

Even the temperature of the room begins to rise as the two counter each other.

"He killed your friend, didn't you just say that?" Hakeem asks. "You are so quick to forgive and think your system will fix him after he caused your friend to be murdered for speaking out against his behavior. You want to fix the behavior of a person who is willing to kill to continue his behavior. That is your call to action?"

"Isn't that what your whole religion is based on?" Jamar questions. "Didn't Jesus preach about forgiveness, casting the first stone, Jonah, Moses, Simon, Father forgive them? Your whole religion is about forgiveness and second chances. Yet with your own people, you don't know how to forgive and provide a second chance."

"Is something going on between you two?" I ask as Jamar walks out of the room and slams the door.

"You don't want to know," Hakeem answers, looking at his phone to avoid eye contact.

"I need to know," I say as he looks at me, then back at his cell phone.

"Jamar and I grew up together, our parents raised us the best they could, but we still fell victim to the streets. We were a part of the Ridgely Homes Gang, the gang people call the Alphas now. We tried to hide our dirt from the streets and from our parents. My father being a big name pastor in the city, didn't need to hear about his two boys gangbanging and selling drugs. One day we spent up the money we were supposed to give to Dom; he was one of the heads of the Ridgely Homes Gang. We got into a shootout with one of

Dom's people that was coming at us for being short on the money. Police caught Jamar hiding with a gun and a few grams of crack cocaine, figuring he had something to do with the shootout. I went to college and did something productive with my life; Jamar found Islam in prison and served his time."

"You serve your God just like Hakeem serves his; why does it sound like you are minimizing his beliefs?" I ask as Hakeem shrugs his shoulders.

"We were raised as Christians, it's hard to explain," Hakeem answers.

"You ever think Jamar sees the community and people like Milk getting the second chance you got when he did the prison time you could have both been sentenced? You clearly got a second chance at life, going to college and being a community leader. Your brother has a felony record that will follow him for the rest of his life."

"No. This community doesn't need to be segregated. That is hate speech that his head was filled with inside the prison." Hakeem abruptly stops talking and walks out the door.

Chapter 11

A few hours after a very unproductive meeting with Hakeem and Jamar I find myself walking into the soundstage area with Gina, who is accompanied by Lela. Lela, still wearing the same outfit from when we first met, looks completely uncomfortable as Anna Cartwright, and her assistant approach us with microphones to place on our clothes. Anna's assistant encourages Lela to "speak normally, the microphone will pick up everything."

I notice Lela and Gina talking among themselves as Anna gazes at my hand tapping my left leg, unbeknownst to me. "Are you ok?" she asks, and I stop the tapping.

"I'm ok, just have a lot on my mind," I answer. There are too many worlds colliding, between this documentary that I somehow got sucked into, my children, Bell, Milk, and Hakeem. Way too much drama. The assistant points at Anna, and she begins the intro to the documentary and introduces Lela. A million thoughts flood my mind, including the fact that I barely know Lela.

"Lela, tell us a little about yourself," Anna asks. Lela leans to her side, then re-postures herself.

"My name is Lela Wall, I'm 20 years old. About six years ago I was kidnapped at gunpoint from my parents in Seattle, Washington," Lela says with a stern look and postures towards

Anna. "The gang called the Alphas took me in, moved me from city-to-city, state-to-state, and prostituted me. They drugged me and some other girls, and kept us at hotels. We would stay near airports, truck stops, casinos and near state capitals for a couple of weeks before changing locations."

"Oh my God, that's horrible," Gina whispers to herself as the rest of us sit in silence.

"I don't remember, or know how I got to Baltimore. I remember being in Texas, New Mexico, Las Vegas, and a few other states. They drugged us so much, to the point that we wanted to be high. They made us feel dependent on them, and we agreed to do what they wanted."

"Can you tell us who the 'we' and the 'they' are?" Anna asks.

"I apologize, the 'we' are the girls that they keep in the hotels, they pack us in the rooms five or six in a room. The 'they' are the Alphas. They keep guards to watch the rooms, and around the hotels. The senior girls have roles; they are supposed to groom and provide treats, that's what they call the drugs, for the girls that perform well. The senior girls are also supposed to punish, dress and feed the new girls. The senior girls place the new girls on eating schedules, they get one decent meal every three days. Every other meal the new girls have to earn. Everything is earned."

"Why haven't you gone to the police?" Anna asks as Lela looks on with confusion.

"Dom, the man that was in charge of us and moved us around was killed by a guy named Milk. Milk is protected by the other Alphas and a group of police that wears all black military-style clothes. They drive unmarked cars and are everywhere. So to answer your question, we can't trust the police, that's why. We also don't have the means to communicate. If we did, I would have gone back home. I haven't seen or heard from my family in years. They probably think I am dead. I had two children. The oldest was killed by Dom to punish me for being pregnant while working. The other was taken. I don't know if she is alive or dead."

"What was her name?" Anna probs.

"I never named the first child. I was not allowed to have an emotional attachment to the second child, so I never named her," Lela says, looking away for a moment, breaking her stare with Anna.

The air in the building feels light. There is a feeling of unease and tension coming from everyone the more Lela speaks. I have concerns and fear at this moment. We already poked the hornet's nest, and are targeted by the Alphas, now we are discussing them being in a sex trafficking ring. They know where I live, they know where my children go to school. I do not have the stomach for this. Is this worth it? I have already lost one child, is it worth putting the other four in danger? Am I a coward? What would my grandmother do? She would fight!

"How did you find Gina and Tiffany?" Anna asks

"They moved us to an abandoned building in the Old Market Place District because there was a tip about a sex ring bust at the surrounding area hotels. I snuck out one night, stayed with a guy in an old milk factory for a few days, saw this documentary he was watching, and happened to bump into them when I went to a counseling support group," Lela answers.

"Was this guy that you stayed with a person you knew?" Gina asks

"No. I met him one day trying to figure out how I was going to get home. He was nice. I mean, I earned my place to stay there for the last few nights. I'm just trying to figure out how can I get home."

"What do you mean by 'earned' your place to stay there for the last few nights?" Anna asks.

"I had sex with him," Lela answers.

"Sex for shelter," Gina interjects.

"Exactly," Lela confirms.

"Can you tell me more about sex for shelter?" Anna asks.

"When I was a sex worker and homeless it was something I did. Sometimes you don't have the money for a place to stay, but there are other means to secure housing. It might provide you a night to stay somewhere, sometimes longer," Gina answers.

"Yeah, I'm trying my best not to do any more sex work. And I'm scared of going to the hotels here in Baltimore at this point," Lela states as Gina's eyes light up.

"Is it because of Hollywood?" Gina asks

"Yes! You know him?" Lela asks with a shocked look.

"When I was doing sex work, Hollywood was one of the lieutenants of the Alphas. He watched the girls that stayed at the hotels. They said he was a part of NAFA as well, like he was undercover. Can't confirm or deny it," Gina answers as Anna looks at me with an astonished look.

"Let's take a break and talk for a little bit," Anna says as Clair walks close to the sound stage.

Chapter 12

Anna, Gina, and I are meeting with Clair inside her large office. The office is decorated with awards, framed records, pictures of celebrities, and degrees on the wall. Separating Clair from Anna, Gina, and me is a massive mahogany-stained wooden desk, with two Emmy awards sitting on opposite sides of the desk. On the window ledge near several colorful plants is a picture of Clair hugging a man, but his face is covered with a sad face sticker. Behind Gina, Anna, and I is a glass wall, where we can see directly into an office where Lela is sitting, reading a magazine.

"Anna, Gina, I'm loving what you all are doing with this documentary. The views are up, and you have created a lot of traffic for the app. The problem is, the direction you're headed in now, with what Lela just said, you won't be able to go back," Clair states, looking only at Anna.

"What do you mean?" Anna asks with her hand on Gina's knee as a gesture of comfort. Gina appears very nervous. Rightfully so, this is the same office her friend, Silk Diamond sat in the day she was fired.

Silk was a radio personality for one of Clair's radio stations, and was one of the first transgender radio personalities in Baltimore. She was suspected of being fired for sleeping with Clair's husband. I think we can guess, the man covered with the sad face sticker is Clair's ex-husband. Case solved.

"When you started the documentary, you discussed Gina's life and her struggles with addiction and being a prostitute—" Clair begins when my aunt interjects,

"Sex worker."

"Sex worker, my apologies," Clair says, looking at Gina before redirecting her gaze at Anna. Clair is stoic, all business and very confident. Even her apologies make it feel like she is right. "Since talking about Gina's history as a sex worker, an addict, a mother and a wife, we have discussed gangs, crooked police officers and now sex trafficking. At this point, we will need more documented proof to avoid lawsuits, and some protection if what Gina and Lela have said is true. Furthermore, when this episode airs, expect an investigation and charges to be made."

"Clair, you know I was a district attorney, I understand how the law works. A lot better than most people," Anna responds sharply. The two share a strong look for a brief moment. Clearly there are two strong egos in this office. Anna continues,

"Clair, there are abuse of power charges, sex trafficking charges, along with drug trafficking and distribution, and racketeering. That's just what I picked up from Gina's and Lela's interviews. What happens when we start locking some of these people up? We're talking state and federal charges here."

"If you get them in court," I interject. "My kids are in danger, Sasha is in danger. My aunt Gina is in danger. Lela is in danger. I'm in danger." I catch myself breathing hard as everyone is looking at me. I realize I was talking very loud and fast.

"Are you ok?" Gina asks, genuinely concerned.

"No, I'm not. I had Bell inside my home, threatening me one night ago. Not only him, but I had one of the Alpha bosses, Milk, trying to stash bags of pills in my yard. My kids play in my yard. When this documentary airs, what will happen next? I can't afford another place to live; I inherited my current house. Where will Sasha live? My kids go to school, they won't be safe, the Alphas will try to kill them for sure."

"Can you prove Bell was in your house and was trying to get you to stash drugs for Milk?" Anna asks looking at me with a stern expression.

I pull out my phone, go to my photo app, and begin playing a recording of the conversation Bell had with me in the kitchen. Bell did not know I recorded the whole conversation, starting with the interaction between Milk and me. Anna and Clair look at each other in silence, but it appears as if they have a full conversation with their eyes.

"Gina, what can you tell us about the Alphas?" Clair asks.

"I used heroin and crack, a lot of times I purchased drugs through an Alpha member. I witnessed with my own eyes NAFA officers raiding non-Alpha gang members' houses, getting drugs and giving them to Alpha gang members," Gina stops talking as Anna asks,

"How can you be sure or prove that?"

"Because they used me to set up the non-Alpha gang members prior to their raids. Either Bell or some other NAFA officers would give me money or a couple grams to do something to get the attention of non-Alpha gang members, enticing them to let their guard down. They had me set up Cabal gang members all the time."

"That's all hearsay," Anna responds.

"I have video recordings on my phone of NAFA officers zip tying non-Alpha gang members in cars and setting them on fire.

"That's a smoking gun," Anna responds. "Let's start making some calls."

"Can I go home first to talk to Sasha and get my kids?" I ask. Anna nods her approval.

Chapter 13

Walking into the kitchen of my home I notice Sasha sitting down and drinking a beer. This is the first time I've ever seen her drink inside the house. I begin to say something about her drinking in the house when I suddenly stop and think about recent events with Milk and Bell.

"You don't have to say it, your face says it all. You don't like me drinking in your house. I get it. This was your grandmother's house and she was super religious. I just didn't want to get shot today because of the shit your aunt got us in."

"Excuse me?" I say as Sasha shrugs her shoulders.

"We're targeted by them niggas because of that documentary your aunt been recording. You then had me on there like I'm some sad case or stray dog in need of some help. You had that self-righteous cop that killed my son on there as some surprise guest to say, 'I'm sorry but,' like that meant something. Do you have any idea what I've been going through, Tiffany? My son was murdered for following after a kid that bullied him, someone he felt powerless against. He was a good kid. Then I had to go on that show and talk about that, only for you to have that cop come out and attempt to justify why he murdered my son, *to my face*. But it's all good, right? Because he a part of the story y'all trying to tell about the ratchetness of NAFA."

"Sasha, I'm sorry," I attempt to interject. Sasha is seriously angry; I've never seen her like this.

"No, you're not. You're blessed. God blessed you with five beautiful children. He took one from you because of a hit-and-run. Your grandmother left you a beautiful house. You had a beautiful funeral for your youngest daughter, you have a family member trying to connect with you. You know what I have? Voids! I have holes in my life. My son's father is locked up for the rest of his life. My son has been murdered by the police. I had a hand-me-down funeral, I have become a spectacle. I'm living in your house. I am alienated from my family because they are religious and I had a baby at a young age. I chose to live the glamorous, fast money life with my baby father, and when he was caught, it all ended. It was me and my son, Ty, struggling. But it was cool because I was putting myself through school. Then Titan Industries decided to purchase the apartment building, which led to me losing my voucher and being homeless. But thank God for my blessed friend Tiffany to the rescue. Her and her four surviving children."

"I'm sorry, Sasha, I didn't mean to cause you no pain."

"You know what's painful? What's insulting? I have nothing to show for my life. My pictures of my son are in a box. His bedroom, his belongings, everything is in a dumpster now because Titan destroyed the apartment building. The media made it impossible for me to get into my own unit after my son was murdered. But I was supposed to be happy that he was a damn hashtag. Hurray, #BlackLivesMatter. How about this one #BlackGriefIsReal. With everything going on, my son being dead, me not at work, me not in school, speaking on the documentary, you know what really sucks? I come home… sorry, I come to your home every day to watch God spit in my face by watching you neglect your four surviving kids. I have me, myself and I, you have four kids, and they are suffering. Why won't you talk to them about how they feel, Tiffany? Because you're scared they will express the same feelings I just threw in your face."

"You think I neglect my children?" I ask as Desha walks into the kitchen with tears in her eyes.

"Every day Desha comes to me crying about not being able to talk to her sister Kenya. She is sad that she used to pick on her and call her stupid. Every day Desha talks about not being able to spend time with her cousin Tina, that used to babysit them. They should be talking to *you* about that. Your children have feelings, Tiffany. You've been spending all that time with your aunt while I have been the person talking to them. This is why I dropped out of school and haven't been to work. I've been filling in the gap you left."

I'm not sure if I should be mad or thankful. Everything Sasha said is true. I attempt to hug Sasha, but she pushes me away and walks out the kitchen into the living room area, leaving me alone with Desha.

"Mom, Aunt Sasha said you love us and you miss Kenya too, is that true?" Desha asks.

"Yes, very true," I answer, reaching out to cup her pretty brown face. "Tell me how you feel though."

"I feel alone. Kenya used to laugh at my jokes, and she used to make funny faces when we watched wrestling. She would imitate the wrestlers when they talked; it was super funny. Mr. Keyon promised to take us to watch wrestling one day before he died. I know you don't like it, but it was something we all used to like watching and doing," Desha says, holding my hand with tears in her eyes.

"I'm sorry, Desha, we can all go to watch wrestling the next time they are in Baltimore," I respond, but she shakes her head no.

"I don't like watching wrestling anymore. It makes me remember Kenya, and that makes me too sad," Desha counters to my surprise. "I don't know what I like doing, anymore."

Searching for the words to say, I pause and hug my oldest daughter. "Have you talked to Darrin, Trinity or RJ about this?"

"No," Desha answers, but I know this is something I can't avoid. I never took into account how seriously this could have affected them. Sasha was completely right. I have to figure out how to fix this situation.

"Is it ok if I go to sleep?" Desha asks. I nod yes. She clinches me tightly and walks away.

After I watch Desha ascend the steps, I walk down into the basement and sit on an old couch, surrounded by boxes, comforters, toys, pictures and random clutter that my grandmother left behind. I take a deep breath, and I hear a voice – my grandmother's voice. It sounds very real, but I know it is in my head.

"Tiffany, you have to do better," my grandmother Florence says. "You are the matriarch of this family now. This house is more than a place to stay, it is a symbol. It has been in our family for generations. This house was built by my great grandfather. I left it to you, not just for the kids to have a place to stay, but for you to have one less thing to worry about while you finish college and lead. You have to lead this family and this community."

"How am I supposed to lead this community, Grandma? I can't even effectively help my children through their grief," I tell her.

"This don't happen overnight, child. Stop trying to do everything right now. Focus on those beautiful kids. They need you today. Hakeem and Jamar can fix their problems without you. The community was falling apart when I was alive, and it will not get fixed overnight. Take a break with Gina as well. I'm proud of you for forgiving her and trying to get close to her. But that does not mean you need to get caught up in her foolishness. That whole documentary thing, it has done nothing but make you a target."

"It sure has," a deep voice says, as a I see a thin-framed man appear before me. He has curly hair and an undershirt shirt that displays his muscles. It is my father, Cube.

"What do you want?" my grandmother asks him.

"What's best for my dear daughter. We don't want her to fail again, like she normally does. Why do you always have to harass me, Florence Simms?" my father asks.

"Because you're a rapist, child molesting piece of garbage. Did the police find you yet, or are you still on the run?" my grandmother asks.

"I'm proud of you," a third voice says. This voice is a soft, scared woman's voice. It is my mother.

As the three voices argue with each other I notice the clock shows the time as 12:34 a.m. No matter how much time I spend in the basement, it always appears 12:34 a.m. on the clock. The time my grandmother died in the hospital. I think to myself how much time has gone by, and ask why I am in an argument with voices in my head. I cannot keep doing this. My father's voice just puts me down, and haunts me.

I walk away, and as I walk up the stairs I can still hear the three fictional voices argue in the basement. As I walk into the kitchen I hear a faint knock on the front door. I think to myself, *Is that a hallucination or is that real?* I crack the door open to find Bell standing on the other side of the door wearing all black and a bulletproof vest.

"I hope I'm not disturbing you, just wanted to talk," he says with a warm smile on his face. He steps back, allowing me space to open the door wider and step outside. Almost everyone has gone inside their house, aside from the Alphas that stand at the end of the block, smoking weed and listening to music on their phones. A man is walking his dog on the opposite side of the street; he looks at Bell, then looks away quickly. An older model jade-colored Jaguar is parked across the street with the engine running.

"You run everything. How can I help you?" I ask, pushing the record button on my phone, and sliding it into my pocket without him noticing. The jade-colored Jaguar drove up the street slowly.

"I just want to make sure you thought about our offer. I think it's very fair. A few dollars a day, we provide you and your family protection. On top of all of that, you don't have to worry about any of the Alphas stashing anything in your yard. Your kids get to have a normal life, you get to have a normal life, we all get to move forward."

"Where am I supposed to get that money from?"

"You're a very beautiful and smart woman. I'm sure you can figure that out pretty quick. Before I go, I just want to warn you about the company you keep."

I feel the air in my lungs escape as he says those words. He is going to kill me for what Lela said. No, he won't, that episode hasn't aired yet. He must know that we know about Lela and the sex trafficking ring. Maybe I should pay him the money.

"Tiffany, you're a good person. Your boyfriend, Hakeem, is a good man. My line of work doesn't afford me to be around a lot of good people, not for leisure. You don't want to keep mixing yourself up in all of this," Bell says with a smile still on his face. Why does this freaking guy look so good? He's adorable but so intimidating.

"What do you mean?" I ask, admiring his smile and his teeth.

"You're not dumb. Leave your aunt alone. I get that you lost a lot over the last year, between your youngest daughter, your grandmother and your cousin, but your aunt Gina is going to be the death of you. Your kids don't need that. God forbid, one of your kids gets caught up in all of this. How will you be able to cope with the loss of two kids?"

"Are you threatening my kids?" I ask. His smile widens but he shakes his head no, moving backwards to provide more distance.

"No. I'm not here to threaten or harm you in any way. But the Alphas are a different animal. I've seen these guys call the cops reporting someone has a gun just so we will search the person on the street. After we drive away because the guy wasn't armed or wanted, a few minutes later they kill him. Horrible stuff."

"Who searched him?"

"It was me," Bell says, slightly moving his face away from me but cutting his eye at me with a smirk. I know what that look and statement means. He wasn't going to kill me, but he had no problem being the person setting up the murder.

"Stay away from my aunt, I got it," I respond.

"That would be your best bet. Good night, Ms. Gibbons," Bell says, walking away. He pauses his exit on the bottom step in front of my home, and looks back at me.

"What?" I immediately respond. I'm not sure if he is going to kill me or kidnap me. He's literally the most dangerous man in Ridgely Square, and I just came off annoyed with this person. What am I thinking? I can feel the air escaping my lungs in anticipation of what he is about to say. He still has a smile on his face, looking me directly into my eyes.

"This whole thing your aunt is trying to do with the documentary or news story. It's not going to work out the way you think it will. Even if you all get enough traction with this story for me to go to court, my silent partner will shut this whole thing down," Bell says as he continues walking out of my yard.

"Who is your silent partner?" I call out to him. He laughs loudly.

"I'm the detective, Ms. Gibbons. That's for me to know and you to never find out."

Chapter 14

The next day I find myself at the community resource center with Jamar with the goal of smoothing out the relationship between him and his brother, Hakeem. It's cold in the community center but hot outside with an odd overcast. There's an eerie feeling outside, a feeling that you pick up on before something bad happens around the neighborhood. I'm in one of the rooms where they store school supplies and clothes for neighborhood children in need. It's a large room with a massive chalkboard adjacent to the windows. A projector is right above my head as I stand in the middle of the room. The room smells like fresh paint, and chalk. Jamar is standing to my left, looking at an inventory sheet.

"Lela will need protection if she does the interview," I blurt out as Jamar breaks his attention from the clipboard and looks at me. "The Alphas are involved in this sex trafficking ring, and if we can expose them, we can get rid of them and NAFA. But we can't have Lela exposed."

"I might have somewhere she can stay at. It's in the county with the family of one of my friends. Nobody will harm her there," Jamar explains, putting the clipboard on a desk. It's a small desk, probably used to belong to a middle school. There's tons of carved artwork and phrases on the desk.

"With your idea of the community doing its own policing, do you think the department will have the ability to fight against sex trafficking to keep situations like this from happening?" I ask as he turns towards me.

"That's what I anticipate. Picture the police being a stakeholder in the community. The people of the police department are members of our community, our neighbors. If something happens, they answer to us. If something doesn't happen, they answer to us. If there's sex trafficking, and one of the members of that force is a part of the sex trafficking ring, they answer to us."

"So do we lock that person up?" I ask. Jamar looks at me with an optimistic glimmer in his eyes. I know this look because Hakeem has the same expression when he speaks about the community.

"We will administer our own judgment. I know this may sound crazy, but we can't trust the criminal justice system, which has failed us for centuries, to do right by us just because we have control of a community. We can turn one of these buildings that have been abandoned into a holding center."

"Are you suggesting that we have our own prison?"

"I think it will have to be determined case-by-case, Tiffany. Even in our own detention center, we offer real reform. We provide therapy, education, and career training to change the offender. Each of those interventions would be home grown, from our community. Everyone is accountable for our community."

"What happens when we think we have reformed a person, like a sex trafficker, but they get out and do it again? Do we go back and do that type of intervention again?"

"We explore how we failed that person, we adjust and we improve."

"What happens when that person gets out again and does the same behavior again? They keep racking up victims and they continue with the same behavior. Are we failing them or our community at that point?"

"You ask the right questions, Tiffany. Your grandmother would be proud. I do subscribe to Florence Simms's and Pastor Donald Avery's theory of community involvement in decision-making. That being said, we would all have to come together to make those types of decisions."

"I like how that sounds. Why is it you and Hakeem don't see eye-to-eye on anything? It's exhausting hearing you two go at it. What happened?" I ask as Jamar picks up the clipboard and sits on the desk.

"I'm sure you know I was locked up for a period of time," Jamar states. I nod my head. "During that time I lost the support of my parents, and time with my daughter. Her mother moved to Florida and has not had any contact with me since then. My father, who's a big-name reverend here in Baltimore, spent more time publicly shaming me in his sermons than actually checking on me. I never understood how you could preach a message about a prodigal son, but leave your own son to die."

"What about you and Hakeem, though?"

"After I got out of that incarceration, I was out looking for employment. My father wouldn't give me a job at the church and wouldn't help by giving me a letter of recommendation to any job I applied for. He went out of his way to tell one employer 'he is not my son.' At the same time, he was telling me I had to get out of the house. Hakeem, of course, was getting all of the love and attention from our dear old dad. So I went back to the old habit of selling crack, which led to me being locked up again."

"I'm confused, this sounds more like your father is the problem, than your brother. Why do you dislike Hakeem so much?" I ask as Jamar stands up and walks towards the window. He stands in silence for a moment, looking out the window at the parking lot and the traffic driving by.

"I love Hakeem, I don't resent him. I resent what he received in contrast to what I didn't get," Jamar answers with his back towards me, still looking out the window.

"What is that?" I ask as he turns towards me at an angle before walking back and forth in the room.

"Grace! A second chance! Our father ostracized me from the family, the church and all of his friends because of my history with selling drugs. Hakeem used to sell as well, the only difference was he didn't get caught. Hakeem was short all the time on our money. We sold for two guys, Dom and Van. Hakeem would blow his re-up money all the time, which will get you killed. I would cover for him and give my portion of the money to Dom and Van. The first time I got caught selling, I had Hakeem's stash of drugs on me."

Jamar stops walking for a second, glances out the window and turns towards me to continue, "The second time I got caught, we were walking together. I saw this group of cops in an unmarked car, coming from a distance. I asked Hakeem to give me his work, so we both wouldn't go to prison. When the car pulled up with the plain clothed police officers, they searched Hakeem and me. Hakeem was sent home, I was sent back to prison. Do you think Hakeem looks back on that event as what saved him, and allowed him to be the preacher and community leader he is? You think he looks at me as the big brother that helped him to become successful when we both were going down the same path? No. I get the same thing from him that I get from our father.”

“I totally get your frustration now,” I state as Jamar turns in my direction, but casts his eyes at my feet. His eyes appear to have tears in them, and he looks very vulnerable for a moment, before he walks back towards the window with his back towards me. Jamar exhales loudly, which I interpret as a giant burden finally being lifted from his shoulders.

“Our father has always pit us against each other. Hakeem and I played sports, Hakeem got all the praise. Hakeem and I made the honor roll, Hakeem got all the praise. Hakeem would always get new clothes, Hakeem got a new bed, new TV, shoes, video games, you name it. Even down to a birthday cake. Hakeem got, and my father went out of his way to show favoritism towards Hakeem.”

“What do you mean, a birthday cake?” I ask as Jamar shakes his head.

“My parents would go to the DeLuca Bistro and Bakery every year and get Hakeem a fresh cake. Every year my mom would bake my cake,” Jamar answers.

“Did you ever say anything?”

“Just once, I was maybe 13 years old, my daddy slapped me and told me to stop complaining, people would kill to get what we had.

I never complained again," Jamar clarified while we both stood silently.

"Years ago my grandmother told me, fight the battles you can win, and fix the relationships you can repair. You couldn't win in the battles against your father, but you can repair the relationship with your brother," I say as Jamar continues to look away in silence.

"Tiffany," Jamar says as the tone in his voice gets deeper, "If Bell and Milk are trying to use your house to stash drugs and want you to pay for protection, maybe you're going to need to protect yourself."

"How?" I ask.

"Have Hakeem stay at your house and purchase a firearm. I'm going to have a couple of the brothers from my mosque drive by throughout the night to look at the house. If they see anything fishy, they will help." Jamar walks towards a long old beat up desk in a corner, and opens one of the drawers. It makes a loud screeching sound as the drawer opens. He then walks towards me and hands me something wrapped in a hand towel. I open the towel and see a small silver revolver. I instantly try to give it back, but he stops me.

"I can't take this," I plead as he shakes his head.

"Protect yourself by any means necessary. You have four children that will need you around. You have to protect, educate and mold those children of yours. You can't do that in a grave. Take this. If you don't have to use it, perfect."

I place the small handgun into the pocket of my jeans and nod at Jamar. I'm shocked by the weight of the handgun, and that it's small enough to fit completely in my pocket.

"Word of advice, if you pull the trigger, breathe and pull it slowly. Never hold your breath and do not rush your shot," Jamar says, looking away from me.

Chapter 15

Walking home from the community center, I notice nobody is outside, which is odd considering the weather. There's an odd overcast of clouds, but the temperature is very hot. Normally there's a group of kids riding bikes, or playing basketball at one of the nearby basketball courts. There isn't a person outside getting drunk, nobody nodding from being intoxicated by heroin. Nothing. As I process the emptiness of the Ridgley Square streets during this time of day, I notice a person slumped over on the steps in front of my house. I open the gate and slowly approach to find it's Hakeem. He is lying on one of the middle steps holding his side and has several fresh bruises.

"What happened?" I call out to him in a panic.

"It was Milk," he says in a low tone. His face displays a lot of pain and anguish. He is barely moving, and breathing heavily. "Milk jumped me with a couple of the Alphas, and then shot me in the side. Can you call an ambulance? They also stole my phone and wallet."

As I grab my cell phone out of my purse and dial 9-1-1, I notice a SUV has pulled up in front of my house. "Yes, my name is Tiffany Gibbons, and I want to report an assault and shooting. The victim is lying on my steps outside," I shout into the phone as the door to the SUV opens and Bell steps out, wearing black BDU style pants, black boots, a black T-shirt and a black bulletproof vest. The dispatcher assures me that someone is en route. I watch as Milk exits the passenger side of the SUV and walks over to Bell and they saunter together into my yard.

"Funny how gang activity leads to bad things happening, isn't it," Bell says in a condescending tone, looking at me with a smile on his face. "This guy right here joins a gang and gets shot."

"Hakeem isn't a part of nobody's gang," I holler at Bell, thinking to pull the gun out of my pocket and shoot him.

"Ma'am, I'm going to have to ask you to stand back and clear away from my crime scene," Bell demands with a smile on his face.

"The guy who shot him is your friend Milk, standing right next to you," I say as a rebuttal.

"There you go, trying to tell me how to do my job. First you and your aunt start this stupid news story slash fake documentary. Next, I have internal affairs doing an investigation into my work. All I wanted to do was make this stupid community safe, and make enough money to get my mother in treatment. What do I get for my efforts? A bunch of ungrateful people. I created a balance where normal people don't get hurt or killed. Did any of your community leaders do that? How about this guy?" Bell asks, pointing at Hakeem, whose legs are writhing in pain.

"Can you please leave? The ambulance is on the way," I tell them, fearful of what he and Milk will do next. I can feel my heart beating faster and my hands are trembling.

"Ms. Gibbons, this is an active crime scene, and this gentleman is under arrest," Bell says, smiling as he places a knee on Hakeem's thigh. He rolls Hakeem on his right side, glancing at the gunshot wound on his abdomen, then rolls him back on his stomach. Bell then handcuffs Hakeem and pulls out a small handheld police radio, requesting for a different ambulance to come to my address, and demands that the dispatcher disregard the previous call I made.

"What are you arresting him for, are you crazy?" I ask as Bell goes into one of the pockets of his BDU-style pants and produces 3 sandwich bags filled with pills.

"Possession with the intent to distribute a controlled substance," Bell answers as Milk walks closer to my house. I can hear the sirens from the ambulance in the distance.

"Stay out of our business," Milk shouts, pointing a small black gun at me. "Stop talking on that documentary and tell your aunt Gina, we're looking for her." Milk nods to Bell and walks away as the red and white ambulance arrives at the front of my house.

Chapter 16

My front yard is in total chaos, complete with police officers and news reporters. Inside my house is no different. Sasha is in the living room area with my daughter Trinity. Sasha and I haven't spoken to each other since the night she talked Desha's grief. Sasha is wearing jeans with manufactured holes in the leg areas and a faded t-shirt that reads "Believe."

"You have to find Gina," she shouts, walking past me to the kitchen area, leaving me in the room with Trinity. "The Alphas will not stop until they get her. This is insanity. You and your aunt dragged me into this. I agreed to live with you, not die for you."

"Aunt Gina came in the house and left a note for you," Trinity says in a low voice. She reaches into her pocket and reveals a note, handwritten by my aunt.

The note states that Gina is in a safe place, and she was warned that the Alphas and NAFA were looking for her. It says for me to go to Tina's hiding place. My cousin's hiding place used to be in the basement, the area where I tend to go and lose track of time. I leave the company of Trinity and Sasha, who is shouting at me, to go to the basement. I enter the area I normally go to for alone time. There I see the clock that reads 12:34, along with a small safe. I never noticed the small safe before. I attempt to open the safe, but it's locked. I use my cousin's birthdate, it doesn't open. I use my aunt's birthdate, it doesn't open. I use my birthdate, it doesn't open. I use my uncle Larry's birthdate, it does not open. What the hell is the combination to this safe?

"Try using 1-2-34," I hear in my ear, which I interpret as my grandmother's voice. I use that combination and the safe unlocks. Inside the safe is Gina's phone and 2 flash drives. I look at Gina's phone and I see multiple videos. The first video is of Bell in the front yard last night. The second video is of the conversation I had with Bell in the kitchen a few days ago. The third video is a meeting Bell had with the Alphas. I watch as Bell and members of NAFA drop off trash bags filled with prescription pills in exchange for money. Gina recorded the whole thing. I briefly watched a fourth video with Bell and several members of the Alphas shooting an officer named Hollywood. How did Gina record and get this into the basement? I walk towards the laundry area to find the back door unlocked. Pissed for a moment that Gina would put my children in danger by leaving the door unlocked, I lock the door. I look back at the phone and see an alert that "the new video has been uploaded to the cloud storage drive."

I start the new video and soon realize it is a full recording of the assault on Hakeem, including the shooting and Bell giving instructions to the Alphas prior to my arrival. I wince at the brutality I'm witnessing and feel even worse now for Hakeem. Seconds later I receive a notification of a series of text messages from an unknown number.

Take this to Anna Cartwright, the first text message reads. I'm hoping to say goodbye to my daughter Tina one last time at the cemetery, the second reads. Bell and the Alphas are out for blood, I don't think I'm going to survive this, the third text message reads.

A few moments go by and I receive a final text message from the same number,

I can't say I'm sorry enough for how I treated you during my addiction. I love you so much, and I'm so proud of the woman you've grown up to be. When I look at you I see what Tina was going to be, and it makes me smile. It hurts that she didn't get the chance to live up to her full potential. A large part of that was because of my actions. I live with that burden daily. Thank you for taking the time to bond with me over the last few months. I love you.

Your favorite aunt,

Gina

I leave out the back door and walk to the Amber Walker Cemetery. The sirens and commotion from the front yard can still be heard has I walk through the back alleys towards the cemetery. The same cemetery where my grandmother, daughter, baby's father and Tina are buried. My heart is beating rapidly, and I'm having difficulty concentrating while thinking about my aunt and what could happen to her while there's so much going on with NAFA and the Alphas. I arrive at the cemetery to see it is crowded with several police cars. Did Bell send these officers after Gina? What if he found out I snuck out the basement and sent them after me? The cemetery's grass clearly hasn't been cut in some time and is growing wildly in some areas. My eyes begin to water as I fear something terrible has happened to Gina.

A black Ford Explorer pulls up on my right side. It is Anna Cartwright telling me to get inside. I enter the rear passenger side door, very appreciative of the air conditioning but concerned about what she will tell me about Gina. Anna has folders and milk crates filled with documents that accompany me in the back seat. In the front seat is a chubby white male with short brown hair.

"Tiffany Gibbons, I would like to introduce you to Agent Dennis Parker. He's an investigator for the FBI and has been following the case with NAFA for a few weeks," Anna states while parking her vehicle on the grass of the cemetery. "Tiffany is the niece of Gina Simms."

"Where is my aunt?" I ask, ignoring the introduction. Anna and the agent turn in my direction.

"Ms. Simms is in a safe place," Agent Parker says to me. He has a very direct tone to his voice. My heart rate continues to increase. I do not feel safe around all these police and FBI agents.

"What about Lela?" I ask, fearing for the young lady's life.

"We currently have her being prepped for family reunification. She is safe and her parents are en route to Maryland," Agent Parker answers. "I cannot provide any further information other than that because of the ongoing investigation related to her case."

"Have you locked up Bell?" I ask as I watch police officers comb the cemetery. "He just shot Hakeem Andrews on my front steps. Bell was trying to plant drugs on him and demanded I go inside my house."

"No, we didn't lock Bell up yet. We're working on that as we speak. Our agents were monitoring the situation and we will have him in custody shortly." Agent Parker states, while turning back to look out the window. "Your aunt said that she left you with two flash drives and a phone. Can you please give them to me?"

"What's on the flash drives?" I ask. I'm not sure whether to trust him or not. He is an FBI agent, but I am still unsure if I can trust the FBI. To be honest, the FBI has not been too trusting of the black community.

"From what your aunt said, she took them from Bell a few months ago when she had him set up rival gang members."

"You can trust him, hun," Anna interjects, noticing my caution towards the agent. I hand him the two flash drives and the phone.

"When can I see my aunt?" I ask. Maybe I should have asked that before I gave over the evidence I had.

"We have her in a safe location. We have to protect her, at least until after the case is decided. I cannot tell you how long it will be. There's a lot of moving pieces involved, including the arrest of Bell, participating members of the Narcotics and Firearms Task Force, and the Alphas. We might have to move you, your children and your partner to a safe place as well," Agent Parker says in a dry tone.

"Sasha is my roommate not my girlfriend," I respond defensively.

"I'm talking about your boyfriend. Hakeem Andrews. The person that was shot earlier on your doorstep. I was trying to be respectful. Some people don't like boyfriend/girlfriend terms, wasn't sure if you were engaged. Partner appeared more respectful." Agent Parker says while exiting the car. He closes the door and walks towards the other FBI agents and a couple of police cars located near a grave plot.

"Off the record, Officer Moreland has been following Bell for a few days, and he recorded the incident that happened at your house last night. He also saved Gina's life here. Prior to you getting here they found his body slightly past where that group of unmarked cars are parked," Anna says in a somber tone, pointing to the far end of the cemetery. More unmarked cars enter the cemetery along with a helicopter that is flying overhead shining a spotlight. The overcast appears to darken around us outside, and the little sunlight that we did have has begun to set.

"What do you mean 'he saved Gina's life'?" I ask, feeling a heavy weight on my chest thinking about the death of Officer Moreland.

"From what I was able to gather, Bell was tracking Gina. He knew she was near your house. He and the Alphas attacked your boyfriend, such a childish term, and he was alerted that Gina was seen walking through the cemetery. Moreland tried to intercept Bell before he could harm Gina. The two had an altercation here at the cemetery. Bell shot Moreland several times, leaving him to die. A person walking through the cemetery saw the altercation and called it in. Moreland hung on long enough to provide a statement, confirming it was Bell that shot him before succumbing to his wounds. He also wanted to say he was sorry to Sasha in his final statements."

"How did you find my aunt?" I ask. The tone in Anna's voice changes to more of a nonchalant tone.

"She was running for dear life and Agent Parker picked her up. She told him everything about the flash drives, the documentary, and about your friend Lela."

Agent Parker knocks on the window of the SUV, requesting that I lower it, startling both Anna and me.

"They caught Bell and two other NAFA officers about to leave from your house. We have units locking up known members of the Alpha gang right now. Would you like an escort to see your boyfriend at the hospital?" Agent Parker asks. He smirks when saying boyfriend.

"Just call him Hakeem. After hearing you say boyfriend out loud, it does sound stupid coming from an adult."

"Would you be open to providing us with a statement prior to your ride to the hospital?" Agent Parker asks, and I agree.

I exit Anna's Ford Explorer and enter a large black GMC SUV. The windows are completely tinted, and the interior is a beige color. There is a female agent and the State's Attorney, Jada Austin standing nearby. Jada is a very tall, muscular dark-brown-skinned woman. Jada's father was once a Maryland State's Attorney, and her grandfather was once the mayor of Baltimore. Jada's mother was a deputy police chief in Baltimore and held office as a city counselor for several years. I've heard rumors that in the past that Jada worked out with professional wrestlers and bodybuilders, and trained in Mixed Martial Arts while in law school.

"Good evening, Ms. Gibbons, is it ok if I ride with you and chat a bit? Then we'll head to my office and I'll ask you a couple of questions," Jada says with a strong and imposing voice.

"Yes, of course," I answer.

"Good, I'll audio and video record the conversation, if that is ok," she says. I nod to show my agreement.

Chapter 17

A few hours later, after going to the District State's Attorney's office, and meeting with Jada, I finally make it to the Ridgley Square Hospital. A tall, heavyset, older police officer walks in front of me as an escort. I stop for a moment and look at a room in the Intensive Care Unit, a room that my grandmother stayed in over a year ago. While looking in that room, I picture my mother, my cousin Tina and my youngest daughter, Kenya. I notice them laughing and talking in the room, and think of the life I wish my daughter had.

My daughter died with her father when they were in a head-on crash with a hit-and-run driver. Kenya's father, Keyon was a good man. He made some mistakes, but he loved his daughter, and he loved me. I loved him too, but our views of responsibility were vastly different. Keyon would sit home, smoke weed and play video games, knowing we had bills and needed groceries at the apartment. He would be unemployed for long periods of time and never attempt to look for a job. I didn't have that luxury. I had to raise five kids, I had schoolwork, I had bills, and I had the cloud of my rapist father hanging over my head. Constantly raining on me. I had to protect the children from the predators in the world like my father. My mother enabled my father and protected him.

The only refuge I had from him was my grandmother. The brightest light in our family. When Uncle Larry was murdered while being robbed, my parents took in Tina, Uncle Larry and Aunt Gina's daughter. I feel like it was my fault my father raped her, and she committed suicide. If I would have told the police what happened years ago, instead of just telling my mother, Tina would still be alive. If I would have told my elementary school, middle school or high school teachers what happened, Tina would still be alive. If I would have stabbed my dad, Tina would still be alive. If I would have told one of the guys in the neighborhood what happened to me as a child, Tina would still be alive.

I don't feel responsible for my daughter's death, the hit-and-run happened. Kenya was with her father, and a bad person did a bad thing. It's hard to accept that, but I do. I stood in this hallway, talking to Tina the day it happened and received the phone call about Keyon and Kenya. I stood in this hallway with Tina and said my final words to her, not knowing she would commit suicide after I rushed to the emergency room to check on Keyon and Kenya. I feel responsible for that. I feel responsible because I did not check on how Tina was processing what my father did. I feel responsible for not telling someone to help me before it got to Tina. I feel responsible because I wasn't in a financial place to take Tina in to protect her when she was in need. The cloud of my father that stays above my head, it rained, it drowned Tina. The depression, the guilt, the burden, the pain. I know those feelings. Being looked at, being judged. Being powerless. It drowned her. In this hallway, I could have saved her, but instead, I ran to the emergency room.

"Ms. Gibbons," the officer calls, bringing me back to myself. He beckons for me to follow him. I stop looking at the hospital room. The images of Tina, Kenya and my grandmother vanish. Oddly I can now feel the air of the hospital. It is cold here. I can smell the hospital, the bleach, and the stench from bowels coming out of a nearby room.

I continue to follow him until I arrive at a room with two other police officers standing outside the door. Both officers are looking down at their smartphones, one with a smile on his face, as he texts someone. The second officer is playing a card game on his phone. I hear laughter coming from inside the hospital room. The escorting officer opens the door and the curtain in the room, revealing Hakeem lying in bed hooked up to several machines. To his left, sitting near the window and facing him is Jamar. The two are sharing a long laugh before shifting my direction with giant smiles on their faces. They look exactly alike.

"Hey, what did I miss?" I ask. They lock eyes and begin laughing again. This brings happiness to my heart. For several years, Hakeem and Jamar's differences stopped them from having these kinds of moments. I just wish this moment wasn't held in a hospital room.

"We were catching up," Hakeem answers. He still appears to be in pain, but is in good spirits. "We were talking about Dad, and how bad he was at sports."

Jamar laughs hard, and Hakeem joins him in the laughter. "When we were little, I was in 3rd grade, Dad coached our team," Jamar begins, trying to catch his breath from laughing so hard. Several medical personnel walk past Hakeem's room with inquisitive stares about the loud laughter coming from the ICU room.

Jamar continues, "We lost every game that season. We found new ways to lose. After every game, the teams lined up to shake hands and high five. After we lost the 5th game of that season, you know what our dad said?" Jamar asks, laughing as Hakeem laughs louder with the look of pain and happiness on his face.

"We'll get them next time?" I question more than answer. The two laugh together at me, almost in tears.

The two brothers respond in unison, "He said, 'No! Don't shake their hands and accept that kind of abuse.'"

Hakeem stops laughing for a moment and holds his side and adjusts the large medical bed to sit up higher. He turns in my direction and the smile reappears. "Our father ordered our team to not shake anybody's hand until we won a game."

"We didn't win a game for two seasons under my father's leadership," Jamar interjects. "He wanted to run and rule everything. If you did one thing that worked, something that he didn't instruct, he would put you on the bench. He used to fight with the parents, the other coaches, and the referees. We would be losing by 30 points and he would fight with parents of the other teams for making too much noise. All kinds of dumb stuff."

"Yeah, he definitely left much to be desired as a coach. Remember how he treated Mom?" Hakeem asks. Jamar stops laughing.

"I honestly believe she was raised like that," Jamar answers. "Their marriage was arranged by their parents because of their status with the church. Her parents were pastors and his father was a bishop."

"That doesn't explain why she never said anything," Hakeem responds.

"Mom was super submissive. Dad was all about control, do as he said, and everything had to look a particular way. Mom was raised to bend to the will of her husband. To be a homemaker. No matter how right you or I were in any situation growing up, Mom made it a point to guide the conversation to what Dad said and how he felt. When anything happened at the church, she made it a point that everyone agreed to what he said or how he felt.

"Everything was a competition with our father, and he was always the one that was going to win, no matter what," Hakeem says, looking at me.

"That's too much," I say looking down, thinking about my own father and mother. Thinking about how my mother was very submissive to my father, to the point she did not protect her children.

"Outside of church," Hakeem begins, "my father sucked. He was two different people. There was the Reverend Bishop Dr. Hakeem Andrews, and then there was Dad. He never went by senior or the first, and never called me junior. He was just Bishop Andrews. He was connected with judges, elected officials, school teachers and everyone else. He would do for everybody in his church but put his own children at odds with each other."

"He even put our adopted sister Kesha at odds with Hakeem and I," Jamar adds.

"Why?" I ask, trying to understand the logic.

"Competition," Jamar answers. "Our father loved competition and splitting people. He loved feeling better than everyone else. He and Pastor Donald Avery got into it all the time. To the point that Pastor Avery stopped dealing with him altogether."

"That is very true," Hakeem says, chuckling. "Pastor Avery and I had a great relationship, and he expressed concerns about my father. He even wanted to know why I didn't want to take over my father's church."

"Why didn't you want to take over your father's church?" I ask, really lost in this conversation.

"I can't follow in his footsteps," Hakeem answers. "My father was a nightmare. He was verbally abusive, manipulative and emotionally dead to the people that were closest to him. Dr. Andrews was a character, and our father knew how to play that role. Our mother knew how to play the supporting cast role. We were victims of the image our father tried to portray. So many issues Jamar, Kesha, and I have to this day are because of the splitting our father did," Hakeem says as Jamar places his hand on Hakeem's leg.

"We'll get through it," Jamar says, looking his brother in the face with a warm smile. "I don't say it enough, but I love you. What happened to us as kids carried too much weight in our lives. We can figure this out."

"We let too much time pass before getting here," Hakeem responds. "We spend so much time helping others, and we don't really help ourselves. I guess that's the real lesson we learned from Dad. It's a shame that it took getting here to realize it."

"Time is an enemy to all of us," I insert into the heartwarming moment. "You can't stop it. No matter what you do, you keep being thrust forward into the next second and moment of life. Before you know it, you have a trail of could have done that, should have done this and would have done something different, behind you. I'm guilty of it too. I spent so much time with my aunt Gina and her drama with NAFA, working here at this hospital, going to school, along with trying to help Sasha, I lost track of my children."

"It's not too late for you to fix that," Hakeem responds. He's such a good man. Very genuine, very loving, forgiving, and open. He has always been very good to my children. The only person that was ever as good as Hakeem to my children was Keyon.

"What's next for you?" Jamar asks.

"What do you mean? I'm going to try to be there and support my kids. I lost my youngest daughter last year, we still haven't overcome that," I answer as Jamar shakes his head from left to right.

"No," Jamar responds with clarification, "I mean with this case. The police are stationed outside of this room. What happens next? We all know Milk shot Hakeem and has been involved with the Alphas. What do you think the state's attorney will do?"

"She's pursuing charges. We're definitely going to court," I answer.

Chapter 18

A few months have gone by, and we are headed towards a cold winter. It's a frigid, yet sunny December day in Baltimore. Last year this time, I was in and out the hospital with my grandmother. This year, I have been in and out the courthouse with my aunt Gina over the NAFA case. Right before Thanksgiving, we had a grand jury hearing for Bell, during which we were not allowed to listen to the interviews. All we know is that it led to this court case. Bell denied having a jury trial, but agreed to have the judge, Donavan Truman, preside over the court case proceedings. Judge Truman was a former police officer, who later became a judge. Judge Truman is a middle-aged African American male with no facial hair, and graying short hair on top of his head. He appears to be tall and bulky.

The actual trial started off with fireworks, beginning with whether or not they should charge Bell with first-degree or second-degree murder for the death of Officer Moreland. Then they argued over whether they should charge him with manslaughter or second-degree murder for his death. Needless to say, he is facing second-degree murder charges, in addition to racketeering charges. They added in a couple of attempted murder charges and assault charges to his case. A member of the Alphas took a plea deal for the murder of Hollywood. The public was upset that they grouped everything related to Bell into this one case but felt that State's Attorney Jada Austin had the public's interest in mind.

The police have assigned a detail to our house for protection from Bell, NAFA and the Alphas. Oddly, since Bell was charged, the crime rate has gone down in Ridgely Square. Sasha and I have not spoken in months. Bell was allowed to return home during the bail hearing and the grand jury hearing. Gina testified yesterday in this now two-week-old court case. She is currently in witness protection. I am scheduled to speak later this morning. The air is brisk in the room, which houses several wooden pews. There's a long mural of what appears to be American lawmakers in the early 1800s that extends across the top half of the courtroom's walls. Paintings of two Caucasian judges from the early 1900s sit to the left and the right of the judge's bench.

To my left I see State's Attorney Jada Austin walk past her table that holds several folders stacked high, and a pitcher of water. To my right I see Bell and a lawyer, an average height Caucasian white male with blonde hair and a clean cut. I was told Bell attempted to fire his lawyer after the first day of trial, but the judge ordered him to keep the lawyer. Bell has decided to represent himself as counsel, and have his lawyer serve in the role of advisor. On the stand is the broadly built, bald-headed former police chief, Alex Tillman, who sports a thick mustache.

"Chief Tillman," State's Attorney Austin begins, "how would you describe Officer Bell?"

"He is a brilliant man," Alex Tillman answers. "He was promoted because of his genius. He saw things in a way that many others didn't and I thought promoting him to the Narcotics and Firearms Task Force team was a great idea."

"During that time did you ever have any concerns about Sergeant Bell's behavior?" Attorney Austin asks.

"Yes," Chief Tillman states, as Bell's lawyer, Gary Rude, screams his objection.

"Overruled," Judge Truman says. "Proceed with your answer, Chief Tillman."

"Yes. He's had a couple of accusations leveled against him related to inappropriate behavior and abuse of power," Chief Tillman responds.

"How did you handle the accusations?" Attorney Austin questions.

"I viewed Sergeant Bell like he was a son of mine. At first I was in denial about the accusations. After a while I looked around to see who was eligible for promotion, someone that could keep an eye on Sergeant Bell. The person that came to mind was Officer Edward Carter. He was another young man I felt was like a son to me. We had an open door of communication. I was going to move Officer Carter to NAFA to work with Sergeant Bell. I met with Carter a few times about the move. I was there with Officer Carter the day he was murdered. It's still hard to process his death."

"What did you do after Officer Carter was murdered in regards to the alleged behavior related to Bell?" Attorney Austin asks as Chief Tillman locks eyes with Bell.

"I met with Sergeant Bell, told him about my concerns, and told him he needs to fly right. Like I said, Sergeant Bell was like a son to me. I always felt we had a great level of respect for each other," Chief Tillman answers.

Attorney Austin returns to her table as Sergeant Bell stands up to walk towards Chief Tillman. His lawyer can be heard disagreeing with Bell about proceeding with questioning. Bell smiles at him and then looks at Chief Tillman.

"Chief," Sergeant Bell begins, "would you say that I had a history of violence when you were in charge?"

"No, not at all. I personally thought a lot of you, " Chief Tillman answers. Bell has a large grin on his face. I have a sick feeling in my stomach, partially because I do not want to answer questions from Bell on a witness stand. The other reason is I hate courtrooms.

"If you could paint a picture of me for this courtroom, what would it look like?" Bell asks, turning towards the gallery with a smile on his face and his arms extended wide apart, as if he were posing.

"You were a great guy. You had a positive attitude, you were well read, and eager to learn. I always felt that you could have done great things. I really thought the accusations would stop, especially around the time of the Kennard Lyles-Bey's and Tyrone Clinton's deaths. One of the major reasons I stepped down was because I saw some of the letters of complaint that came across my desk, and knew this would be bad. I couldn't have asked you to step down because your numbers, at least on paper, were great. Your unit was making arrests and getting convictions. Getting really bad people off the streets. Outstanding work. But with everything going on, and the accusations against you and your unit, it was just a matter of time before it would have hit the fan. Officer Carter would have been a great person to guide you in the right direction. It's a shame that never had a chance to happen."

"No further questions," Bell says as Chief Tillman shakes his head from side to side, steps down and walks out of the courtroom quietly.

"Your honor," Attorney Rude says in a high-pitched voice, "against my better judgment, the defense would like to call its next witness, Sergeant Marshawn Bell."

Truly surprised by this because I figured I would be called next, I lean forward in my seat with intrigue. How will this play out, I wonder. Why does it seem like Bell doesn't care how this case goes? He has butchered his whole case, poorly questioning people and allowing State's Attorney Jada Austin to have her way. Does Bell understand that his freedom is on the line? Bell approaches the stand, and he is sworn in to speak.

"Sergeant Bell," Attorney Rude begins in a cracking, high-pitched voice, "can you please tell the court about your upbringing?"

"Objection, your honor, what does this have to do with the case at hand?" State's Attorney Austin says, standing at her table next to several large, burgundy-colored folders. The folders appear to have documents spilling out of them.

"Overruled," Judge Truman says, leaning back in his chair, glancing at Bell.

Bell leans forward in his chair, then rocks back with a large smile on his face. He makes eye contact with me before looking at Attorney Austin. "I grew up in Baltimore City. I lived with my parents and younger brother. My father was abusive. He would beat on my mother, my special needs brother and me. One day my mother made breakfast for my father, my brother and me. We were sitting down at the table. Price Is Right was being played on the TV in the living room. We had one of those really heavy large console TVs that sat on the floor, and you could put stuff on top, like pictures and other decor. This was the late 1970s or early 1980s, mind you. Anyway, my father had just slapped my mother moments earlier for taking too long making the breakfast. My mother got up from the table, left the room for a moment and then came back. We all were still eating, not thinking much about it. My mom said, 'I got some good news and bad news. The good news is I slept with your brother, the bad news is you have to die.' My father's brother, Uncle Leroy, walked into the kitchen with a gun and shot and killed my father. My mother and Uncle Leroy rolled my father up in a large floor rug, wrapped it in chains and placed it on the back of a pickup truck. I learned later that they tied cinderblocks to the rolled up carpet and dropped my father's body in the Chesapeake Bay."

"What happened to your uncle Leroy?" Attorney Rude asks, scratching his head with a look of discomfort about the subject.

Bell leans back in his chair, still with a smile on his face, glances in my direction and says, "My mother killed him one day. She used Uncle Leroy's gun, the same one he used to kill my dad, and killed him with it."

"Why?" Attorney Rude asks without hesitation.

"Because my mother caught him beating my brother with a long wooden stirring spoon. My brother Tyler is special needs. He's not very verbal, has a low IQ, and does not comprehend a lot of things you and I take for granted. You can reprimand Tyler, but abusing him with a wooden stirring spoon, that's a bit much. My mother went to one of those hardware stores, I think called Hechinger, purchased a tarp, two saws, chains and cinder blocks, and came home. She and I began sawing my uncle apart, at the legs and arms. We wrapped him in the tarp, then in a large blanket. We chained the blanket and tried to take him out on the boat she went out on before when she dumped my dad's body. When that didn't work, she and I went for a ride to South Carolina to a small town. We found a rundown house and placed the body inside it."

"Did your mother say anything to you during this time, or did you know what to do?" Attorney Rude asks. Both his mouth and eyes are wide open in shock. I don't think he knew Bell would tell this story. The rest of the courtroom sat in silence. I felt the hairs on my neck standing up and I was very concerned.

"She told me that family takes care of family no matter what," Sergeant Bell says. "She told me that she loved my brother and me and that she would do anything to protect and provide for us. My mother also taught me that is what I am to do for my brother and for her. She made me believe that we always have to care for each other, no matter the cost. My mother was a school teacher; I watched her work two jobs at a time to provide for us. When it was time for me to work, I made sure the money came to the house. I never purchased stupid stuff like the expensive shoes or video games other guys would buy. I would purchase stuff for the house, making sure my brother was ok, and my mom didn't have to worry about all of the bills."

"What made you become a police officer?" Attorney Rude asks, completely at a loss for words.

"I wanted a career. When you're in high school and about to graduate, they tell you 'go to college and get a good career.' Nobody ever tells you what those good careers are. When you're from where I'm from, you know the police are harassing you for being black, the person at the grocery store, nurses, and teachers. You don't see people that look like me working in computers, or doing psychology, or working on medical equipment like an ultrasound. You don't think that stuff is open to you. Like some of my friends got jobs out in Hunt Valley doing telemarketing, I didn't see a future in that. I needed to provide for my home. So I did what was safe and guaranteed: police work. I started the job on my 21st birthday and never looked back."

"No further questions, your honor," Attorney Rude says as State's Attorney Austin approaches the witness stand, looking at a smiling Bell. The tension in the courtroom is very high.

"Sergeant Marshawn Bell," State's Attorney Austin begins.

"That's my name, don't wear it out," Sergeant Bell responds with a large smile and chuckle.

"Can you tell me about your life in high school? Not having a father or father figure must have been rough," State's Attorney Austin asks with a stoic look on her face.

"Objection, she's leading the witness," Attorney Rude yells.

The judge agrees with the objection and State's Attorney Austin nods her head in agreement. "Sergeant Bell, what was school like for you?"

"I was bullied a lot until I began working out. A lot of the kids in the school were a part of gangs and knew each other for years. My mother didn't allow me to hang out with a lot of the kids in the neighborhoods we lived in. We frequently moved because of the money challenges my mother faced. Why?" Bell asks with a smile on his face.

"Sergeant Bell, you're on trial for murder, racketeering, assault, and—" Attorney Austin abruptly stops her line of questioning when Bell begins to laugh loudly.

"I brought balance. I brought balance to the Ridgely Square community and to Baltimore City. There was a reduction in the murders of innocent people. There were fewer assaults on innocent people. The people that were murdered, robbed, and hurt deserved it. I controlled the problems."

"Objection!" Attorney Rude yells, but the judge denies it.

"Can you elaborate?" Attorney Austin asks with a stone cold look on her face.

"Yes I can," Sergeant Bell says grinning. I wonder if he has lost his mind. Bell appears to have admitted to his actions after giving a not guilty plea at the beginning of this trial. Is he trying to sabotage his whole case?

"There were so many people walking the streets with multiple murder convictions, terrorizing this city. Destroying property values. Hell, in Ridgely Square now a group of outside developers called Titan Industries are trying to gentrify that area. Why? Because of what is happening from the same courthouse I stand in today. Bad people walking. I controlled the bad people on the street from doing bad things to good people. This is how I am thanked. On trial. What happens while I'm on trial? More bad people walk the streets doing bad things, this time to good people. You know why? No balance with the checks. The prison system isn't designed to help people get out and find a job. No, it helps the state. Those inmates make lottery tickets for the state, scratch-offs, documents for the MVA, fix state vehicles, and a lot of other garbage. When those inmates get out of prison, they can't get a job with any of the skills the state provides."

"Objection, your honor!" Attorney Rude screams.

"Shut the hell up," Sergeant Bell screams back and then he laughs for a second. "I created a system. A system that benefited the people and allowed me to provide for my mother, to get the help she needed."

"What about your brother?" Attorney Austin asks.

"My brother was taken by Adult Protective Services right after I received charges from the state. I haven't seen him since," Sergeant Bell says with a smirk still on his face.

"Can I ask you why you are smiling so much?" Attorney Austin asks as Bell leans back in his chair, and then slouches in the chair.

"I'm about to walk out of here a free man," Sergeant Bell answers. "I gave the heads of the Alphas trash bags filled with prescription pills as payment for the murder of Officer Edward Carter because I knew Chief Tillman was going to use him to spy on me. I told them exactly where he was going to be in the hospital, and how to get in there unseen during the riots. I'm telling this to you because I'm going to walk out of here a free man."

"How is that?" Attorney Austin ponders aloud.

"My silent partner agreed with my methods because it made us all look good. The last thing my silent partner would want is for everything to look bad for them, when we all benefited from this," Sergeant Bell says in a low tone and a smile.

"Your honor, I would like to request that my client be psychologically tested," Attorney Rude shouts while standing up, both hands on his desk.

"Your honor, may Counselor Rude and I approach the bench?" Attorney Austin asks.

A loud white noise fills the courtroom as the state's attorney, Jada Austin, and the defense attorney, Gary Rude walk to the bench to speak to Judge Truman. A few minutes go by as Attorney Rude signals for Sergeant Bell to come back to the table with him.

"After speaking with the prosecutor and the defense, it has come to my attention that the defendant, Sergeant Marshawn Bell will be a key witness in a federal trial. In exchange for his testimony, he will be granted clemency for his federal crimes. In coadjuvancy for his cooperation with the federal prosecutor, the state's attorney's office has agreed to drop all charges related to Sergeant Marshawn Bell. I will be granting a restraining order against Sergeant Bell for Tiffany Gibbons, Gina Simms and Sasha Greene. The restraining order will stand indefinitely. Case dismissed."

A large gasp is heard in the courtroom as Bell looks back at everyone in the gallery with a smile on his face. Attorney Rude attempts to speak to Bell as Bell winks and blows kisses to people in the gallery.

Chapter 19

Later that night I walk outside the house, awaiting the arrival of Sasha. During my long day at court and work, I thought about the decline in our long-time friendship the whole day. Sasha and I have been best friends since we were in middle school. We haven't had a meaningful conversation since she spoke and stormed off the set of Anna Cartwright's show. I notice the patrol car that was posted, is driving away from my house as a large black SUV approaches. I also notice the jade-colored Jaguar in the distance. I think to myself they must be unmarked cars for the shift change. There's a cold chill in the air and a large new moon fills the sky. I admire the orange color of the moon, before thinking about Bell and what will happen now that his court case is over. He's a free and dangerous man that feels he is above the law at this point. The rear passenger side door of the SUV opens, and Milk jumps out, pulling Sasha out with him by her hair. The moonlight gives me a clear view of the gun in his free hand. When the front passenger side window rolls down I see Bell in the driver's seat.

"Get in the car, Ms. Gibbons," Bell yells out to me in a playful tone with his signature smile on his face.

"I would rather not. Can you please let Sasha go," I respond.

"Get in the car now," Milk snarls, placing the gun to Sasha's neck as he walks closer to the gate of my front yard.

I can see the air escaping quickly from Milk's mouth and nostrils, because of the extremely low temperature.

"I need you to go for a ride with us," Bell says loudly. "It's important."

"Get out of here before I call the cops," I shout back.

"Ms. Gibbons, I'm not trying to hurt you, I swear. I need you to help my mother," Bell responds, his voice sounds desperate.

"He's not lying," Sasha says. "She's in the back seat and not in good condition."

"Shut up," Milk hollers at Sasha, pulling her head to the left and torquing it so the gun in his right hand can rest against her neck.

"What do you want me to do?" I ask in fear for Sasha and myself. My children are inside, and I also fear that they might see this and become traumatized. I feel flooded with emotions in this moment. I have attempted to protect my children from trauma and bad experiences their whole lives, but it seems they keep following after me, no matter what I do.

"Get in here and help my mother," Bell demands, then quickly softens his tone. "I promise I'll bring you back. I just need you to help get her stable; your friend is too intoxicated to help."

"Fine." I give in reluctantly. "I'll help, but I need Sasha to watch the kids until I get back.

"I'm not going in that house, I am sick of you and your family," Sasha snaps in disgust.

"Go in the house, Sasha," Bell bellows.

"Do what he said," Milk commands, pushing Sasha forcefully.

There is a shot and Milk falls instantly.

Bell, pointing a smoking gun in his right hand and holding the steering wheel in his left screams, "Sasha, go in the house with the kids, *now!* Ms. Gibbons, get in the back seat."

Sasha and I cross paths as she enters the gate. She gives me a very angry look, making me feel uncomfortable. I don't want to fight with her. How did we get to this place as friends? I enter the large SUV and find a woman lying on the back seat, unconscious. I notice several intravenous bags.

"What's wrong with her?" I ask as I get in the back with her and close the door.

"It's my mother," Bell says as he rolls up the windows. I look down at a small-framed woman with very thin hair. She has several dark spots on her skin. Her breathing is shallow, and she is unresponsive to my touch. I look up and notice Bell's somber expression. "I need you to save her," he says in a forceful tone. The smile that was on Bell's face is now gone.

"What do you want me to do? She's not responsive. I'm a certified nurse assistant, not a registered nurse. I don't think I can provide the level of care she needs in this vehicle," I say with concern and fear. I have never seen this look on Bell's face and I'm not sure where he is driving us.

"I need you to keep her stable. We're going to the medical center in Newport News, Virginia," Bell says sharply. "I have some morphine sulfate, dopamine hydrochloride, and saline on the back seat. Just keep my mother stable until we get to the medical center."

"Where did you get this stuff?" I ask with a quiver in my voice. "They don't sell it over the counter." I wonder if I will ever see my children again. Bell just beat his case, the only chance we had at stopping this monster, and now I'm trapped in the car with him. The most unstoppable madman in Baltimore has me in his truck helping his dying mother, while he is driving and not acting like himself. There is no smiling, no laughter, or sarcasm. This is the same guy that was joking in the courtroom a few hours ago.

"A few months ago, I raided a house belonging to rival gang members, I think the Glock Boys or the Cabal. In the house, I zip-tied everyone in the family, except for a guy in a hospice bed. When I saw him, I started searching for prescription drugs. I soon realized that everyone I zip-tied wasn't family. Two of the women were home hospice workers. I took the medication and let them go."

"What did you do with the family?" I ask. Bell looks forward and becomes quiet. "You're about to be a witness in a federal trial and you can't answer my little question?"

"Help my mother," Bell orders, placing his gun on the center console. He looks in the rearview mirror as I tend to his mother, attempting to get a heart rate and blood pressure on her. "I killed them. You happy? I killed the family except the old guy in the hospice bed. I felt like he was going to die anyway."

"I don't remember ever hearing about no case like that, are you lying?" I ask as I try to gauge his mother's temperature.

"The Alphas burned the house down. The old guy in hospice was still alive and defenseless when they did it. It made me feel horrible. I gave the order for them to get rid of the bodies and they did," Bell yells at me. "You think I like doing stuff like this? I don't. I just want to keep my mother and brother alive, and thanks to your aunt, I might not ever see my brother again."

"Your mother needs to go to the hospital," I yell back at him.

"Say it again, and you'll be in the same cemetery your daughter is in. We're not going to a damn hospital. We're going to Virginia to save my mother." Bell's face is etched with both anger and worry. I feel the tears in my eyes trickle down my face at his mention of my youngest daughter.

"I apologize," Bell says, glancing back in the rearview mirror. He quickly refocuses as he turns onto the highway. "I can't lose my mother, and I know you can save her."

"How do you know?" I ask. I am confused and I fear that Bell has lost his grasp on reality.

"You listen, you're not trying to get a handout. You provide for your children at all costs. That's why I like you, Ms. Gibbons. You remind me of my mother. Beautiful, good, protecting, providing, independent. A survivor. I can look and tell you're a survivor." Bell is quiet for a moment. "I'm lying," he says when he speaks again. "I read the case file about your dad. I read what he did to your cousin Tina, Gina's daughter. Pretty bad stuff. One of the cops that shot your roommate's son, Tyrone Clinton, was one of the same ones that took Tina to the hospital after your father sexually assaulted her. Crazy stuff, huh?" Bell says, rubbing his chin with his left hand's pointer finger and thumb.

"I didn't want to bother you tonight. I was going to take Sasha, have her help and then sail off into the sunset. She was too drunk to help though. What's up between you two?" Bell asks.

"I'm not sure," I answer, not liking the idea of sharing personal details with Bell.

"It's something. You did have her son's murderer meet with her on live TV. That's some low stuff," Bell says, glancing back at me, still with a serious tone.

"Maybe. I'm about to start this IV line for the morphine; please try to limit the bumps," I say as he briefly smiles.

"Thanks," Bell says in a soft tone. "You see how you gave that demand? I like that."

"You like what?" I ask.

"You took power back into your life. I've noticed something about you, Ms. Gibbons. You give out so much power; where do you keep your own?"

"What do you mean?" I ask. I'm lost with his logic.

"Never mind. Were you close to Tina Simms?" Bell asks.

"We grew up like sisters," I explain. "Her father was more of a father to me than my own. As you mentioned, my father raped Tina. He also raped me several times while I was growing up. He was abusive as hell. My mom used to defend him every chance she got. My grandmother Florence Simms protected me and raised me. When she was diagnosed with Alzheimer's, I truly felt lonely, like I didn't have a real parent. Tina's father was murdered during a robbery and my grandmother was losing her memory. It was just me and five children. Well, five until the hit-and-run."

"You try to contact your father or have him contact you?" Bell asks as I place the IV bag on the hanger hook by the window next to his mother's head. She is resting on a large pillow and under several blankets.

"No and no," I answer. "I haven't spoken to my father in years." I remember that I have a small revolver in my pocket. I became accustomed to wearing it after Jamar gave it to me a few months back. It's crazy how you get used to the weight. When I got home from court and work I put it in my pocket, and then this craziness happens, being kidnapped by Bell.

"Good, take your power back from your father. He's a scumbag."

"What do you mean by taking power back?" I ask while checking the IV line, ensuring there are no bubbles in the line.

"I don't get into relationships. I have relations, but I don't have relationships. You know why? Because you give up power. I believe power is the most important thing in the world. People drink and get high because they want to lose control, feel free, which makes them give up their power. When you're high, you're not in control, the feeling is in control. When you drink and you feel good, you're not in control, the feeling is. When you do give or take in a relationship or a marriage, you're not in control, the idea of a relationship is in control. The rules that govern the relationship are in control.

"When you have kids, every outside influence in the world is in control. The pediatrician, the schools, social services, lawmakers, the courts, if you aren't with the parent of the child, even the grandparents. But when you don't have kids, do you know what you have? Power. Control. That's why I don't have relationships because I lose the power that I have, and I have to share it with someone else. I have to now adhere to rules and systems that did not apply to me before."

"Do you really believe that?" I question as Bell affirms with a head nod.

"You had a chance to take some power back in your life. You had your four surviving children living with you, no mortgage, no rent. An inherited house. You moved a friend, Sasha, into your home. Then you got into a relationship with Hakeem, and you got involved with your aunt Gina's drama. You gave up so much power. Hakeem wants to do the right thing. Make Ridgely Square a better place and stop the gentrifiers, like Titan Industries. Gina wants to stop the illegal activities. Sasha needed somewhere to stay while she was processing the death of her son. All those things are real issues, but why do you need to be involved? You had the power to help your friend Sasha, who was facing homelessness, so you did. I get that. You wanted to have the power of a community leader like your grandmother, so you started helping your lover, Hakeem."

I laugh, which confuses Bell. "Sorry about that. I recently came to the conclusion that the term "boyfriend" is very childish, so when you said lover, I thought that sounds more mature and less mature at the same time."

The two of us laugh at that statement for a brief moment. "Ms. Gibbons, my mother freed me from my dad. She freed my brother from my uncle. At that moment, I knew what true freedom was. Home. Peace. Nothing else matters. At all costs take care of home and family. Let everything else fix itself."

"What happens after you take your mother to the rehab center in Virginia?" I ask in fear.

"I'm not going back home if that's what you're asking. I just killed a high ranking Alpha member. I'm not going to testify in the federal hearing for the sex trafficking case. Too many big names are involved. I don't want to have any part in that. I'm at the end of the line. I know I have a hit on me by the Alphas, the Glock Boys, the Garcia Familia, the Cabal, and every other gang in the Ridgely Square community. Maybe even Baltimore City's high society group, the Flamingo Club. You need to be to your kids what my mother was to me. A god! A protector, at all costs. That power speech I gave you, take that in."

"Two things: Number one, stop man-splaining to me how I need to be a mom, Number two, I can't do what you're saying because I have responsibilities."

"No, you just *think* you do; you have choices. Your kids are your responsibility. You guys have a home now, not some apartment that Titan Industries purchased and demolished out of spite for black people. Thanks to your grandmother, you are now a homeowner. That makes you a stakeholder and a person with power. Your power is making a better place for those four kids. Not being there for everybody else in the world. Damn them, your kids are most important. Time is short, time is your enemy, and before you know it, time is gone. Use your time for your children so they can remember these times and give more to their children."

"Speaking of time, how did you know you would be free?" I ask Bell. He begins laughing again. Finally, that smile returns, but only briefly before the stern look reappears.

"I had a silent partner, the Baltimore City District State's Attorney Jada Austin. Early on when I started the partnership with NAFA and the Alphas, Jada had some evidence that came across her desk that pinned me into some questionable scenarios. During that time we discussed how we could benefit each other's careers. She became my silent partner. I would give her a financial kickback every two weeks, and she would make sure nothing would ever happen to me. We had a period of time when everything was going good, and then we learned that the Alphas were involved in a sex trafficking ring. We figured we'd see how far up the ladder of important people this sex ring got and use it as a back door to get out of anything that implicated us in anything bad. Of course, your aunt got involved. We met and discussed how to legally protect ourselves and made sure that the federal witness for immunity was on the table. I paid Jada Austin off pretty well for the favor and here we are."

"Why are you telling me all of this?" I inquire, fearing his answer. My stomach feels grossly empty. I don't feel like I can pull my gun on Bell, let alone shoot him. He perfectly shot and killed Milk through the window of a SUV. My chances are very slim.

"That large purse next to you has $7 million in gift cards. Those gift cards are for you. I gave you $1 million per child, including Kenya, and $2 million for yourself. There's a small clutch bag next to the big bag, it has $1 million for Sasha. I did a lot of damage to you all. Like I said, I'm not going back to Baltimore. I want to do right with the little bit of time I have left. I'm going to pay for my mother's treatment. Get my book bag filled with cash and gift cards then disappear. As far as I can get, I'm gone. My brother is in a better place, my mother will be in a better place. I'll make do. That's power."

"Do you want me to say thank you? You shot my…" I pause for a second, knowing I was about to say boyfriend. "You shot my lover."

"That's an abuser mentality; no, I don't want you to say thank you. What I did to you all was never personal. It was all business, Ms. Gibbons. Take the money, keep your mouth closed and live. The Alphas will never bother with your family. Milk is out the picture now, I'm out the picture and you all have too much clout, thanks to the documentary series and the court case. Start over. Buy another house if you want. You have the power to do so now. Be your own person. Your grandmother left you that house and wanted to make Ridgely Square a better place. What if it's not for you to make it a better place? What if you're not in that position to do it yet? Be god to your children, protect and provide for them. Leave the community work to the Hakeem Andrews' of the world."

We ride in silence for a while as I check on his mother and the morphine dripping from the IV line. We soon arrive at a large glass medical facility that has a huge fountain in the front. The facility looks like a sprawling college campus. Bell pulls up to the front of the building and calls out for a staff member to come to the SUV quickly. I find myself standing next to Bell as several staff members run to the car, one pushing a stretcher. The staff members place Bell's mother onto the stretcher as he cries and panics, wearing the book bag that contains his cash and gift cards.

"Come inside with me, I'm going to pay for my mother's stay here. After I'm done, take the SUV back to Ridgely Square and get to your family," Bell says as the jade-colored Jaguar pulls behind us with its high beams on. The driver steps out the car with a gun in his hand pointed at Bell. "What the hell is this?" Bell screams and pushes me out of harm's way moments before being shot several times.

I look past the high beams and notice Alex Tillman holding a gun that still has smoke coming from the barrel. I look down at a lifeless Bell, lying on the ground as staff members of the medical facility run to the door.

"I saw everything, Ms. Gibbons," Alex Tillman calls out to me. "Get in the car, I'm taking you back to your children. You're safe now."

"I left my purse and Sasha's purse in the truck," I call back to him. He nods, and I run and get the purse and the clutch bag filled with gift cards.

"I'm sorry you had to see that. I couldn't let that unstable monster live another second," Alex Tillman says. I discern the trembling of his hands.

"You killed him. You're going to just leave him here?" I ask as Alex Tillman pulls a badge out of his pocket.

"I'm a retired police chief, I'll be ok. I've watched this whole thing to see how it was going to play out. I followed you all from the time he pulled up to your house to now. I knew his mother was in the vehicle and I didn't want to put her in jeopardy."

"He was going to pay for his mother's treatment; he has the money for it in his backpack," I say as the two of us sit in silence thinking about the backpack filled with money and gift cards on the ground next to Bell's body.

"He killed one of my officers, Edward Carter. Just because he didn't want to get caught," Alex Tillman says as the tremors still control his hands. "I loved both of them like my own children. I should have done more back when I first heard Bell was dirty, Edward Carter would still be alive. This is all my fault. I have to make sure nothing like this happens again."

"I knew Edward Carter, he went to my church. He was a good guy. He was a coach too," I say as police cars arrive and we look on in silence.

Chapter 20

It's been a few days since the shooting in Virginia, and I am happy to be back home with the children. Sasha and I are sitting at the round wooden kitchen table. After the conversation with Bell, I thought it would be important to discuss our challenges, instead of letting things get worse. Sasha appears more sober than her usual self, not denying the fact that she may have had a couple of drinks prior to us talking, but she is more coherent than in the past.

"Tiffany, you know what my problem has been for the last few months?" Sasha asks, watching me as I drink from a water bottle. "We met with Anna Cartwright, discussed my son's murder, and I even had to face his murderer. How many times did you come to me and talk about how I felt about it? Anna was judging me for several months after my son was murdered, and you went to her to talk about me."

"Sasha, that wasn't me," I explain. "You can be upset with me about anything you want, but the idea to go to Anna was not on me, that was Gina."

"I felt humiliated though. We live in the same house, but you never once asked me how I felt. I get that you work at the hospital, you have the kids and have your college classes. You offered to take me in the house when Titan Industries closed and leveled my apartment. But somehow it really felt like I meant nothing to you."

"I apologize that you felt that way," I respond as Sasha shakes her head in disagreement.

"I was spiraling out of control with my drinking. You saw me grieving. I get that you wanted me to go to the group you was going to, but I'm not ready for people. I can do 1-to-1, but not groups. I was publicly humiliated by Anna and by that police officer that killed my son. Then I had those dirty cops, along with Bell and Milk hold guns to me. This is too much. I can't do it anymore."

"What do you want?" I ask as I watch Sasha's arms and hands move involuntarily.

"I want to get help. I want to get away from this drama. This city killed my son, and almost killed me. It almost killed your children too. What happens next time? I'm going to stay with Gina for a while and figure things out. You two are my only family. I love the kids. I just have to get away from all of this."

"You want to go to Gina, but get away from the drama?" I ask, feeling surprised.

"I'm going to her place because she is a recovering addict, and she would understand my behaviors. Maybe she can do or say something that will help after she's out of witness protection. I want to go inpatient for treatment as well. I just have to make changes. It's not going to happen here," Sasha says as I look on, confused, saddened that my best friend is moving out and yet, I understand.

"Let's be real, Tiffany. It's too much happening here. The death threats, the documentary, the whole situation with the Alphas. I need a fresh start. I'm still going to babysit the kids and everything. I just need time to figure myself out. Who am I? I know I'm more than the drunk friend, that is a grieving mother. That's how Anna Cartwright portrayed me. You, my best friend, my sister, my roommate, didn't defend me. I am a little hurt and possibly a little bitter about that. But who am I? Who are you? You're the mother of five with four living children, a student, a nursing assistant, now a homeowner and millionaire that no one can know about. But aside from all of that, who are you? You've survived so much trauma from your father, and now from NAFA, does that define you? I don't want any of that trauma to define me. I have let it define me for so long. I have to graduate from it. I want you to do the same. Because I love you, and the trauma you endured has made you a prisoner. I know what goes on in the basement," Sasha continues.

"What goes on in the basement?" I ask.

"You talk to your deceased daughter, grandmother, and cousin. Sometimes I think I hear you talking to your father and mother who are nowhere to be found. You have to get that under control. That trauma and baggage is suffocating you. And just so you know, I don't want that money that Bell gave you for me," Sasha says.

"Why? It's a million dollars," I assert with confusion.

"You think it will buy you freedom. I believe it will make you more of a slave to the abuse and trauma you endured than anything. You got that money the easy way. You chose to get that money when you had an out. He was someone else who forced you to do something that you didn't want to do. I can't be a slave to anyone, not anymore. I need freedom. I value our friendship more than anything. But I can't be a slave to trauma or grief. The groups you were part of, go back to them. Find some way to release. You have been going in too many directions for the last year and it has changed you."

"Thanks," I say before walking over to Sasha and hugging her. "You *better* babysit these kids."

"I will. Not because I'm forced to but because I love doing it," Sasha says, squeezing me tighter. A few moments go by as Sasha hugs the children who are in the living room watching our 55 inch flatscreen television, before leaving the house with a suitcase and some bags.

I sit down next to Desha and Trinity who are watching cartoons. I really don't understand the premise of this cartoon. It's about a cat that wears an eyepatch and fights crime against an overweight rat in a white suit. The kids love it. Darrin and RJ are playing some fantasy role games on the iPad. I smile for a moment and think, How often have I had moments like this since Kenya died? I actually didn't have moments like this when she was alive. I was always working, in college, or in court. RJ's father is incarcerated for murder. Desha and Darrin's father was murdered in prison around the time Trinity started walking. I never talked to them about his death. I used to have alone time with the kids when riding to Jessup, Maryland in the taxi to that prison. I wonder how that has affected them.

"You guys ok?" I ask. Nobody answers me. "I mean since Kenya, Tina, grandma and Keyon died, how have you been doing?"

"Ok, I guess," Desha answers. Desha has always been the leader and the most vocal of my children. She has always been the strongest willed and sometimes the most difficult child. Darrin is more of the aggressive silent type. He backs up Desha, but has developed a closer bond to RJ over the last few years. RJ is more the gamer, and a jokester. Trinity, has been a loner since birth. She attempts to be more like Desha at times, but often goes into her shell. She reminds me so much of myself. Her father is also my dad, and she is a constant reminder of the abuse I endured. Sasha was fearful that I thought I was defined by my trauma. No, I'm actually haunted by it. Trinity not only looks just like me, but she also looks just like my father. It's not easy coming home and being a mom when you look in your child's face and relive your childhood and adult trauma, over and over again. I've been running from my children, and pushing them off on Sasha, while I try to be everything for everybody else. What is wrong with me?

"I really miss grandma's double chocolate cake. I wish I knew how to make it," I say as Desha and Trinity look in my direction. "I really miss Tina's crazy obsession with tennis and the Williams sisters. Most of all, I miss the stories Kenya would make up about dinosaurs eating up my secret stash of chocolate in my bedroom."

"She used to eat my chocolate too," Darrin says as my eyes tear up. "I caught her a few times, and acted like I didn't know what she was doing."

"She was always so hungry," Desha says in an aggressive tone. "Like, who eats that much?"

We all begin laughing and then sit in silence for a moment. Trinity breaks the silence and says, "I miss Mr. Keyon. He used to take naps with all of us."

"He also ate all our snacks," Desha says in an angry tone.

"He also used to buy some of the best snacks to replace the snacks he ate," Darrin responds.

"He was always so sleepy," RJ says in a low tone, turning off the iPad.

"Because he was always high from smoking weed," Trinity says as everyone laughs.

"Let's make a deal," I say, looking at their smiling faces. "Let's make it a point once a week to spend time together and talk. We can get something to eat, like pizza, and talk about the good and bad times. That's what grandma used to do with everyone in the kitchen on Sundays after church."

The kids agreed with me. I suddenly remember I have clothes in the washing machine ready to be put in the dryer. I got distracted when Sasha came over to talk. I walk to the basement thinking about how much time I have missed with my children. I should have had these conversations all along. I should have told Gina no, when she got me involved with Anna. I should have stepped back from Hakeem's and Jamar's family problems. I am glad they have resolved their differences and are working together. I maybe should have taken a break from school. As I step onto the basement floor, I feel cold air flowing, which is odd because I turned the heat up earlier. The children never touch the thermostat. The air feels like it is coming from outside.

I reach in my pocket and feel for the handle of my gun that has now become a regular part of my wardrobe. Having a firm grip on the handle of the revolver, I walk to the back of the basement, where the laundry area and the back door are located. I see the back door has been broken and is standing open. I turn to my right and see a light-skinned, small-framed, unkempt man with a lot of facial hair that appears very familiar. It's my father, and he is a shell of his former self.

"Tiffany, I need your help," he says in a deep voice. The same deep voice that used to torture me. He extends his hand towards me and I back away. His hands, the same hands that assaulted and abused me. The same hands that would give me candy, cakes, chocolates, and toys to keep 'his little secrets.'

"Call the police and be done with this man," I hear my grandmother say in my right ear.

"Tiffany, can you hear me?" my father asks, extending his hand closer towards me as I back up further.

"You remember what he did to me?" I hear Tina saying in my left ear. "Do you remember what he did to us?"

"Forgive him and be done with it," I hear my grandmother plead. "Sasha was right. Don't be a prisoner to him anymore."

"Tiffany!" my father yells, reaching towards me. "Why aren't you listening to me? I need to stay with you for a little bit. It will be like old times."

"Don't let him hurt you, Mom," I hear Kenya's voice say in my right ear.

I pull my gun on him when his fingers lightly graze my chest area. He retreats back towards the wall with a look of shock on his face. I feel overcome with fear. I feel all the hurt, pain, shame, disgust and confusion I used to feel as a child each time my father assaulted me. I remember my mother defending him, and denying what I was saying, as if I would lie.

Next to my father I see a face; no, now I see the whole body of a person wearing all black. He's wearing black combat boots, black BDU style pants, a black t-shirt, a black bulletproof vest, and a badge. He is smiling ear-to-ear, with his beautiful face. It's Marshawn Bell. At this point I know I'm witnessing a full-on delusion because I saw his dead body. Just as I saw my grandmother's, Tina's and Kenya's at the Allen Bradley Funeral Home this time last year.

"Put that away, Tiffany," my father says, reaching his hand closer towards me. I question if he is real until I feel his hand on mine. I yank my hand back and reposition myself with the gun. I discern the fear on my father's face, and finally feel power over him. I have finally taken the power from my father.

"It feels good, doesn't it?" Bell says with a smile on his face. "Remember this moment. Live in this moment. Never let it go. He wants to take from you. The world wants to take from you. This is your house. Your kids are in this house. Protect these kids. Protect yourself. Keep your power. You are free. Stay that way!"

"You don't have to do this," I hear my grandmother whisper in my ear.

"When does it stop, Tiffany? You remember what he did to us, who knows who else he did that to or will do it to. Think of your kids," I hear Tina say in a pleading tone.

Bell places his arm around my father, who is completely unaware of any of these conversations transpiring and continues to smile. "You know he killed that transwoman your aunt Gina used to hang out with. Silk Diamond. She was a personality on the radio before she became homeless. Think about that. Your father raped you and your cousin and was never arrested for it. That is not completely true. Your father was arrested for raping Tina, but the commissioner let him out on his own recognizance. The charges were dropped completely after Tina took her own life. Your father murdered a trans sex worker, and the police department has been looking for him ever since. You saw firsthand how the law works when I was on trial. You saw how I walked away, and I ran a criminal empire. I even admitted what I did in court. You think they'll keep your father? Even if they do, where's the justice for what he did to you? What about what he did to your cousin? Didn't the burden of your father's sexual assault lead to your cousin committing suicide? You're hearing voices and imagining me now because of the effects of the trauma your father put you through. You think calling the cops and having him get the chance to testify in court is fair? Do you want to testify in court about what he did to you? You have the power to change the narrative. He broke into your house. He's a danger to you and your family. What are you going to do? Stop being his victim!"

I begin to smile, and my father looks confused. My father turns to his side for a brief moment, attempting to see what or who I was looking at before making eye contact with me again. As we lock eyes, I see pure fear on his face. The voices stop, Bell disappears and I begin to laugh before hearing a deafening sound.

Bang!

Freedom.

To be continued in *The Legacy.*

Visit www.kylesberkley.com

BOOKS BY THIS AUTHOR

www.amazon.com/stores/Kyle-S.-Berkley/author/B07FK2YRT6

About the Author

Dr. Kyle Berkley is a husband and father from Baltimore, Maryland. After graduating from Fredrick Douglass High School in Baltimore City, Kyle attended Coppin State College with a major in history. During that time Kyle produced and wrote songs for hip hop, R&B, country, and gospel music artists. Kyle would later continue his education at Sojourner Douglass College and Morgan State University, where he earned his Bachelor's and Master's degrees in Social Work. Kyle also earned a Master's degree in Philosophy and a Ph.D. in Human and Social Services from Walden University. In 2012, Kyle and his wife, Rebecca, created a nonprofit organization called the 4 Us Initiative that provides safe housing for victims of domestic violence, homeless families, and preventive care for adolescents.

In 2014, Kyle was elected as a representative to the Baltimore City State Central Committee. Along with serving on the State Central Committee, Kyle has provided mental health therapy, grief counseling, and case management at Baltimore City shelters, hospitals, medical centers, transitional houses, outpatient medical, crisis response teams, The American Red Cross, and substance abuse treatment centers.

Kyle Berkley released his first novel in 2018 entitled *The Wake*. In his free time, Kyle can be found cooking, playing video games with his 3 daughters, enjoying vacation trips with his wife, reading, and watching movies. Kyle is a huge history buff and comic book collector. Kyle also enjoys fishing, playing sports, weight lifting, engaging in casual debates on various subjects, praying, helping people in need, and spending time with his family.

Letter From the Author

I want to give a little disclaimer first. This story is not related to the Gun Trace Task Force. I started working on this story around the time I finished writing *The Wake*. The story kept evolving and that is why it did not comeout in 2018 as planned.

We made it to the end of *The Void!* What a way to end the first book in this series. Tiffany may have freed herself from the shadow of her father, but at what cost? Gina's in witness protection and Sasha is on the outs with Tiffany? Also, the whole Marshawn Bell of it all. What effects did he leave on the community going forward? Let us not forget the actions of former Police Commissioner, Alex Tillman! Where do we go from here? I promise you all are in for a wild and exciting series. Check out the next book, *The Legacy!*

"One of the best Baltimore stories, since *The Wire.*" -Moe Crosby of the Earth 2 Cosmic Cast

"Look what's cooking! If you live in Bmore or not in Bmore, this book is Bmore! Pick it up and read the damn book!" BlakBoxx Radio